PRAISE FOR
CARLTON MELLICK III

"Easily the craziest, weirdest, strangest, funniest, most obscene writer in America."
—*GOTHIC MAGAZINE*

"Carlton Mellick III has the craziest book titles... and the kinkiest fans!"
—CHRISTOPHER MOORE, author of *The Stupidest Angel*

"If you haven't read Mellick you're not nearly perverse enough for the twenty first century."
—JACK KETCHUM, author of *The Girl Next Door*

"Carlton Mellick III is one of bizarro fiction's most talented practitioners, a virtuoso of the surreal, science fictional tale."
—CORY DOCTOROW, author of *Little Brother*

"Bizarre, twisted, and emotionally raw—Carlton Mellick's fiction is the literary equivalent of putting your brain in a blender."
—BRIAN KEENE, author of *The Rising*

"Carlton Mellick III exemplifies the intelligence and wit that lurks between its lurid covers. In a genre where crude titles are an art in themselves, Mellick is a true artist."
—*THE GUARDIAN*

"Just as Pop had Andy Warhol and Dada Tristan Tzara, the bizarro movement has its very own P. T. Barnum-type practitioner. He's the mutton-chopped author of such books as *Electric Jesus Corpse* and *The Menstruating Mall*, the illustrator, editor, and instructor of all things bizarro, and his name is Carlton Mellick III."
—*DETAILS MAGAZINE*

GLASS CHILDREN

CARLTON MELLICK III

ERASERHEAD PRESS

PORTLAND, OREGON

ERASERHEAD PRESS
P.O. BOX 10065
PORTLAND, OR 97296

WWW.ERASERHEADPRESS.COM

ISBN: 978-1-62105-333-0

AUTHOR'S NOTE

I used to think I was fragile and made of glass. But it turns out that the glass I'm made of is actually 1.5" thick plexiglass. It's not easy to shatter plexiglass. The stuff is basically bulletproof. You know, unless the bullets fired are high velocity armor piercing rounds. So even though I'm made of plexiglass I'm still weak to high velocity armor piercing rounds. I guess extreme heat is also a big weakness. I will easily melt in extreme heat. And plexiglass isn't scratch resistant either so I wear my scars where everyone can see them.

So I guess being made of plexiglass means I'm not completely invincible, but at least I'm a lot stronger than I originally thought I was.

Glass Children is my 66th book. I hope you enjoy it.

—Carlton Mellick III 3/29/2023 6:49pm

CHAPTER
ONE

Children these days are made out of glass. They are delicate little things that break easily, even under the slightest of pressures. Their skin is thinner and more brittle than eggshells. Their bodies are empty of muscle or blood or bones, filled instead with a gaseous substance that replaces all bodily functions. They weigh no more than thirteen pounds at their heaviest and can barely hold themselves upright when they walk on their tiny glistening feet.

In order to keep the children alive, they must be handled with the utmost care. Parents must watch over them at all times and protect them from anything that might bring them harm. They must follow their little ones to school every day and guide their every little step. Even a light wind could knock one over and cause their fragile body to crack open if someone wasn't there to catch them with padded pillow-like gloves. And if walking with more than one child, they must be kept at least ten feet apart to prevent them from touching or bumping into each other. Even brushing gently together will create scratches across their smooth glossy surfaces that can never be polished away.

It is very important to keep the children safe from all harm at all times. In order to achieve this, politicians have made new laws to protect the youth from all forms of danger. There are several strict rules for how to take care of the children and how to behave when in their presence. Homes and schools must be completely child-proof. Protective gear must be purchased and always at hand. Every citizen, young and old, has a responsibility to do everything in their power to keep the new generation out of harm's way.

Architects have had to start rethinking how they design cities. Buildings can no longer be constructed with hard materials like wood or concrete. Instead, they are crafted with plastics and soft foam. Sidewalks are now made of rubber padding so that even if the little ones were to fall over they would only bounce in a pleasant jovial manner. Vehicles are now gentle plushy electric carts that are prohibited from accelerating beyond twenty-five miles per hour.

It is a very difficult challenge to keep this new generation from breaking to pieces, but society has no choice. To ensure the future of the human species, every effort must be made to preserve their fragile lives.

Many children do not even survive the birthing process. They often shatter in their mother's womb. Without warning, without rhyme or reason, fetuses will sometimes just burst into pieces. News sites crudely refer to this unfortunate occurrence as *popping*, and it is the thing that all expecting mothers dread more than anything, causing many people to wonder if it's wise to even attempt to start a family at all. Women must take extra precautions while pregnant. They must try to stay as motionless as they possibly can, sometimes staying in bed for the whole nine months with a steady stream of muscle relaxants and painkillers, wearing diapers and taking sponge baths and listening to quiet classical music.

But no matter how careful a woman is, popping happens more commonly than doctors want to admit. Almost half of all pregnancies end with the mother in the hospital, getting shards of glass removed from her uterus. And that is if she is lucky enough to make it to the emergency room in time to be saved from internally bleeding to death. Being a new mother is more horrific and dangerous than it's ever been in human history and it gets only more frightening once the child is born and needs to be protected from the hard, dangerous world we live within.

Nobody knows why the children are made of glass. Some really smart and charismatic people on the news claim that it's due to all the hormones that go into food products these days or chemicals in the atmosphere from all the factories polluting the planet. Others say it's due to the pills and vitamins modern women take to ensure healthy fetal growth. But a few people believe that it's just a natural evolution in response to how society has grown to accommodate the weak and ostracize the strong. Mainstream culture has nurtured fragile and entitled children, coddling them as if they are delicate little flowers instead of preparing them to withstand the harsh world. It's no surprise they have become glass.

Big Bill Mason is one of many citizens of the older generation who is not a fan of all of these changes that are happening to his city. He never had children of his own and hates that other people's kids are the cause of so much cultural upheaval. He had to give up his beloved vintage 1969 Ford Mustang that he had been restoring for two whole decades. He had to give up bowling and drinking and watching baseball on television. He had to tear down his lovely three bedroom Colonial style house that he'd finally paid off and get a whole new mortgage three times that of his old one just to build a much smaller one-room shack made out of rubber and synthetic fluff even though he had no intention of ever letting any kids step foot on his property. And on top of all that, he has now been forced out of retirement to work without pay for the local daycare center that is in desperate need of new staff.

When he received the notice in his mailbox, Big Bill thought it was a joke. There's no way he could be forced to work a job against his will without pay. It is unconstitutional. He's an American. He has rights. But when he called the number of the government office on the paper, they told him he had a patriotic duty to do everything that is asked of him. It is like he's being drafted into the military even though there hasn't been a war in over thirty years. No matter how much he yelled and screamed and complained about the crooked government, they just told him that if he didn't show up at the daycare center on the day he was requested that he would either be fined $150,000 or spend the next ten years in jail. He had no choice but to comply.

Bill is a sixty-eight-year-old man. A veteran. A man who loves his country. But with all these new laws, he's beginning to love his country less and less by the day. He thought the younger generations were supposed to look after him now that he's an old man, not the other way around. He despises the idea of spending the rest of his retirement pampering a bunch of brats just because they're too weak and fragile to take care of themselves. Nature is about the survival of the fittest. If these kids aren't strong enough to survive then it's just Darwinism doing its job. And if the human race dies with them then so be it. It has nothing to do with him. He'd rather just spend the rest of his life in peace, driving his car in the countryside, bowling with his buddies, and fishing for rainbow trout in the creek. All the things he worked so hard to enjoy.

But now Bill finds himself getting ready for his first day on a job he never would've chosen to do. He doesn't own any work clothes anymore. He doesn't have anything fancy or even anything that isn't littered with stains and holes. But he gets dressed in whatever jeans and shirt he can find in the back of the closet that still fit him and don't smell too bad. Then he gets into his little government-approved vehicle that's kind of like a cross between a golf cart and a stuffed animal. The exterior is covered in bright baby blue fuzz to make it look more like some kind of big fluffy cartoon hamster than a car, making for a more pleasant and unscary sight for children who might see him driving by from the sidewalk. His soul dies a little every time he steps inside of this thing. As a man with a passion for quality cars, he can't believe he's been lowered to driving such an abomination. His only consolation is that he was able to get a blue one instead of the bubblegum pink and candy purple cars that are more commonly in stock.

As Bill drives down the padded road at a snail's pace toward the address that he was given, he pulls down his baseball cap so that he doesn't have to deal with looking up at the sky above him. Every day, the atmosphere becomes more and more polluted by a hideous alien smog. A blanket of orange, green and purple swirls blocks out the sun. Even though it's not their fault, Bill blames the glass children for this. Whenever a child is broken, the gases within their bodies leak out and float up into the heavens where they just linger and never dissipate. It is wreaking havoc on the environment, turning rain water into neon-colored poison that is destroying crops and killing fish in the rivers. The news sites say that the rain is perfectly safe to drink and poses no danger to living organisms, but Bill knows better. He knows that it's toxic. He knows that it's not natural. If the Good Lord wanted the world to have rainbow-colored skies then He would have made them that way in the first place. Nothing good will come from the strange gases that grow within the bodies of glass children. And the more children that shatter, the worse it's all going to get.

When Big Bill arrives at the daycare center, he's surprised at the sight of the place. He expected it to be a small rundown house like the daycare center he went to as a child, but this place is a massive state-of-the-art facility the size of a downtown city hospital. Dozens of people are arriving, pulling into the parking garage ten stories high. He follows them in but then discovers that he needs a special permit to get through and decides to just park in the visitor lot out front.

He knows he shouldn't be parked here, but Bill doesn't give a crap about the rules. There's nowhere else to park unless he wants to walk five blocks. Unless they tell him to move it, he's staying put.

The other cars in the visitor's lot belong to parents dropping off their children. They get out of their vehicles and fasten small glass figures into plushy strollers twice the size of grocery carts and filled with cushions.

Although he's ten minutes late, Bill decides to have a cigarette before going inside. He lights up a Marlboro Red, then leans against the fluffy rear bumper of his car and takes a drag. He probably won't be able to have another cigarette for the rest of the day so he plans to enjoy this one while he can.

From the other side of the parking lot, a small glass child begins coughing as Bill takes a puff of tobacco and blows into the air. The child is so far away there's no way that he's coughing on Bill's smoke. But the parents give him a murderous look anyway. Then another child even farther away starts coughing. It's as though just the sight of someone smoking is enough to cause them to react.

After his third drag, a woman in a pink uniform charges toward Bill as though she's ready to hit him across the face with her clipboard.

"Are you crazy?" she yells at him. "Put that out!"

Bill takes a last drag and glares at her as he drops it to the rubber and stomps it out.

"There's no smoking within five miles of the daycare center," she tells him, and then returns to the entrance of the building.

Bill just grumbles and kicks the butt beneath his vehicle.

"Fucking bullshit…" he says under his breath, flipping her off with a warted middle finger when her back is turned.

The second Bill steps through the front doors, he runs right into the woman in the pink uniform who scolded him in the parking lot. It's like she was waiting there for him, sneering at him with her beady eyes and crooked lips.

"Not that way," she says when Bill moves toward the direction of the lobby. "Are you a volunteer?"

Bill faces her, his beer belly filling the space between them. "Hell no, I'm not a volunteer. You think I'd do this shit willingly?"

The woman hushes him and says, "Watch your language. This is a no-swearing zone."

Then she points to a sign on the wall that reads: No-swearing zone.

He scratches his head when he sees it. "Well, if you say so…"

"You have to speak in gentle tones here," she explains. "We expect everyone to create a calming atmosphere for the sake of the children."

She says this in such an angry and annoyed tone that Bill wonders if she shouldn't be following her own rules. After only half a minute in her presence, Bill's more stressed out than he's been in weeks.

"Come this way," she tells him. "Volunteers are supposed to use the side entrance."

Bill doesn't like her using the word *volunteer* again. If they're going to force him to work against his will, they better at least own up to it. Call him a conscript, a slave laborer, or at least an involuntary volunteer. Otherwise, it's offensive.

"There were no signs telling me where to go," Bill explains.

She just shakes her head. "Didn't you read the instructions we sent you?"

Bill shrugs. "I only got a notice to appear here on this date and time. It didn't tell me anything."

She rolls her eyes at him. "You were supposed to check the app. Everything you need to know is on there."

"What app? I wasn't told about no app."

"We announced it on our social media."

"I'm not on social media. Do I look like the kind of guy who wastes his time online?"

"It's your civic duty to follow us on social media. Give me your phone."

Bill hands her a small black device with a cracked screen. It's so old that the woman doesn't even recognize it as a cell phone, holding it with a confused expression like she's trying to figure out a piece of alien technology. Once she realizes that she can't even turn the thing on, assuming the battery must be drained, she hands it back to him and says, "Just download the app and get informed. We don't have time to teach you everything."

The woman opens a door off to the side and leads Bill down a corridor, trying to keep him away from the parents checking in their children at the front desk. She takes him to a much smaller, mostly empty reception area. Standing behind a counter is a woman wearing a puffy neon orange dress and ginger pigtails that make her look like a birthday clown.

"I've got another one for you, Linda," the pink woman says, shoving Bill toward the counter.

She shuts the door behind Bill and leaves him alone with the woman in orange.

"Are you Bill Mason?" Linda asks.

Bill nods. "People call me Big Bill. You know, of Big Bill's Used Cars from a while back. You remember those commercials, don't you?"

The woman ignores him, looking over her paperwork.

He continues, "That was me. Big Bill."

He puts his hands on his hips, puffing out his chest as though he thinks of himself as a little bit of a celebrity in need of recognition. But the woman doesn't seem to care.

"You're late, Mr. Mason," she tells him. "We expect you to show up on time."

"What are you going to do, dock my pay?" He laughs while saying this, even though he means it to be more of a criticism than a joke.

The woman doesn't find it funny. She lets out a sigh. "And I see you're not wearing the appropriate attire. We gave you explicit instructions to wear cheerful colors. Blue jeans and gray shirts are offensive colors to the children."

"I don't own any cheerful clothes," Bill says.

The woman sighs again. "We can provide you with a uniform for today but you'll need to purchase suitable clothing. There's a shop on our app that offers a wide range of styles."

Bill groans. "That app again… What bullshit…"

The woman looks up at his grumpy expression. "Is there a problem, Mr. Mason?"

"Yeah, you could say that. I've got a problem with all of this. Forcing me out of retirement to wipe the asses of a bunch of little shits? Last time I checked we lived in America. Not Nazi Germany."

"We all have to do our part," she says.

"Well, I'm not here to do my part. I'm only here to stay out of jail. If I had the money I would have just paid the $150,000 fine to get out of it like all the tech CEOs in California are doing."

Before he can finish complaining, the clownish woman pushes a clipboard into his face and tells him to fill out the forms. He grumbles as he accepts the clipboard and takes a seat across the room. It's like the woman has been dealing with people like Bill for months and is completely unfazed by it. Bill decides it would be better for his heart to just cool off and sit around for a while. Perhaps if he fills out the paperwork extra slowly he'll have an extra hour or so to relax before having to actually do any work.

After Bill finishes his paperwork, he is escorted to the bathroom where he's forced to change into a bright pink jumpsuit that is ill-fitting and barely buttons up over his gut. He is disturbed by the reflection of himself in the mirror. If his old dad ever saw Bill wearing such a girly outfit when he was alive, he would've beaten him half to death and then burned it in the backyard.

"Are you ready?" the woman in the clownish dress says as he steps out of the bathroom.

Bill shrugs. "Do I look ready?"

"None of the trainers are available right now, so you'll be with me," she says. "I'll show you where you need to go."

As she turns to lead him down the hallway, Bill grabs her by the shoulder. She bristles at his touch.

"Hey, wait a minute," he says, releasing his hand from

her body. "Nobody ever told me what I'm supposed to do."

She turns back to him, smoothing down the section of her dress where Bill's hand had touched.

He says, "I have to warn you, I'm not any good with little kids. They make me uncomfortable. Always have. If you have anything that doesn't involve working directly with them I think that would be best. Cleaning toilets, mopping floors. Whatever you need as long as you keep me away from them."

"I'm sorry, Mr. Mason, but we're going to put you wherever we need you. Your discomfort is none of our concern."

She continues down the hallway. Bill follows.

"You don't understand," he says. "Little kids and me don't mix."

"Then you will be happy to know that this facility doesn't cater to young children. It is a daycare for teenagers between the ages of thirteen and fifteen."

A dumbfounded look stretches across Bill's face. "Teenagers? There's daycare for teenagers?"

The woman nods. "Because of their condition, glass children will need to be looked after for the entirety of their lives. They are too fragile to take care of themselves."

"Are you shitting me?" Bill asks. "What about when they're all adults? How are they going to survive once all the normal humans die off?"

"There is technology being developed to replace human caretakers, but until then it's up to all of us. If we don't do our job properly it will mean the extinction of the human race."

Bill can't help but laugh at her words. He knows she's completely serious, but it all seems like a lost cause. If the glass children will never be able to look after themselves, he doesn't understand why anyone bothers.

CHAPTER
TWO

Bill is brought into a monitoring station where a guy even older than he is sits in a wheelchair at a desk watching security camera footage with an intense gaze. The guy must be in his late eighties, maybe even his nineties. Bill can't believe they're forcing someone of his age to work at this facility. He belongs in a nursing home.

"These are the youths who will be in your care," Linda tells Bill, pointing at the glass children on the monitors. "If we weren't so short-staffed we never would let you interact with the children let alone be responsible for them, but we don't have a choice."

Bill gets a closer look at them, leaning in and squinting his eyes. The screen shows about a dozen or so glass children lying in large fluffy beds surrounded by custom-designed pillows molded to fit their delicate bodies.

"You said these were teenagers," Bill says in a gruff voice. "These ones look no older than six."

Linda nods. "They are all around thirteen years old. Because of their condition, glass children don't grow very large. It's hypothesized that they'll not get much larger than this when fully grown."

"Huh…"

Bill knows that the oldest of the glass children must be around fifteen. It was about that long ago that children started being born made of glass. But he's never seen a teenager before. He assumed they would be teenager-sized, but now that he knows that they all stay the size of little kids he wonders if he's seen more teenage ones than he realized. There could be teenage glass children living on his block for all he knows.

"All you have to do is bring them their meals, make sure they're entertained, keep them happy and peaceful, and make sure they don't try to get out of their beds."

"Keep them happy? I don't even know how to keep myself happy."

"If they have any special requests that you're unable to fulfill you can contact me. Whatever you do, never tell them no. If they want a new toy or device or want you to sing them a song, just tell them you'll be back in a moment. They must get everything that they want or else it could result in a disaster."

When Bill hears this he looks at the clownish woman with a perplexed face. "Are you kidding me? Don't you think that's spoiling them too much?"

Linda shakes her head. "You don't understand. These children are incredibly fragile. Not just physically, but emotionally. If they get stressed out or angry or upset they will tense up and it will cause their glass to crack. It's very dangerous for them to have an emotional flare-up. Here at Sunshine Daycare, our main priority is to keep the children happy and at peace. We will do whatever it takes to ensure they get absolutely everything they could ever possibly want."

"Must be nice," Bill says, laughing and shaking his head.

Linda turns away from the monitors and looks him in the eyes. "This is serious. We have a lot of special cases here that need a lot of attention. A lot of them are in an emotionally fragile state because their parents abandoned them here because they were unable to properly look after them. Others have been cracked and are on the verge of shattering. One misstep, one off-remark, and you might be responsible for killing a child in our care. This is not something that you can take lightly. If you say the wrong thing that results in the death of a child you could spend the rest of your life in prison."

Bill nearly loses his shit when he hears this. "Are you kidding me? You can't let me in with those kids then. I'm only doing this to get out of jail time and you're saying that if I mess up I'll end up there anyway? Sounds like a shit deal."

Linda is beginning to lose her patience. "If you follow our instructions then it won't come to that."

"It's a little much to ask though, isn't it?" Bill asks. "I can't promise I won't mess up. I already said I'm no good with kids. I don't think it's a good idea putting their lives in my hands."

Linda points at the guy in the wheelchair. "Hank here will be watching you on the monitors. He'll let you know if you step out of line."

Bill looks down at the guy in the wheelchair. Hank just grunts at Bill. Bill grunts back. They have an understanding.

Before she turns to leave the room, Linda says, "You have an important job to do. Don't fuck it up."

"If you put me in the same room with kids I'm most certainly going to fuck it up," Bill says.

Linda goes through the doorway. "And there's no swearing here, so watch your language."

"But you just said *don't fuck it up*," Bill says as Linda walks away.

She doesn't respond to him.

Bill lets out a loud groan and leans back. "Jesus Christ Almighty, what in the Sam hell have I gotten myself into…"

In a calm Southerner voice, Hank says, "Should've brought a wheelchair."

Bill looks over at him.

Hank keeps his eyes on the monitor as he says, "They don't make you interact with the kids if you show up in a wheelchair."

Bill's bottom lip flares up. "Are you saying you can walk, oldtimer?"

"Who you calling an oldtimer?" Hank says. "Of course I can walk."

Bill thinks about it for a minute. "I wonder if I still got my old ma's wheelchair in storage…"

"Too late now," Hank says.

"Well, shit…" Bill says, placing his hands on his hips. After a few moments of the two men groaning and grunting, Hank says, "Better get to it. The kids'll get cranky if you don't bring 'em their midmorning snack."

"And where the hell am I supposed to get that?"

"The snack cupboard is across the hall." Hank points through the doorway. "You're responsible for rooms two-fourteen to two-twenty."

Bill nods. "Sounds easy enough."

Hank adds, "My advice though? Start with room two-eighteen. The twins, Tony and Toni, are the most difficult on our block. They're the ones you have to watch out for. The brats get worked up way too easily."

Bill looks over at the storage closet and back to Hank. "Well, thanks for the warning."

Then he gets to work.

In the snack storage, Bill has no idea what he's supposed to do. There are dozens of different brightly-colored boxes of food that he's never heard of before. In his days, a snack would be a granola bar, some peanut butter crackers, or a handful of goldfish. But these foods don't make sense to him whatsoever. They all look like little boxes of cotton balls or tubes of toothpaste. He doesn't have his reading glasses so he's not sure he's got the right stuff. He wonders if he's even in the correct room or accidentally wandered into a cleaning supply closet.

He returns to the monitoring room holding handfuls of blue and pink boxes, and asks Hank, "What the hell am I supposed to give them? I can't make heads or tails of this stuff."

Hank looks over at him for a second and then returns his attention to the monitors. "Just take ten of everything and put them on the cart. Let the kids choose what they want. Give them as much as they ask for."

Bill looks down at the items in his arms and holds up a blue box. The picture on the packaging looks like it's just a wet sponge. "Are you sure this stuff is edible? It looks more like cleaning supplies."

Hanks nods. "It's glass children food. They can't eat normal meals like chicken fried steak or meatloaf, so we feed them this stuff. They like it though. Just give it to 'em."

Bill stares down at another box with a plastic casing. The contents inside are moving around. They appear to be live spiders, but are bright green and made of some kind of gelatinous material. When he sees them crawling around in there, Bill flinches and drops the package on the ground.

"Hey, don't lose anything," Hank says.

"Are those spiders in there?" Bill asks.

Hank shakes his head. "They're bug snacks. They're alive but not real spiders. Biologically engineered. The glass kids love eating live things. Bug snacks are their favorites."

Bill leans down to retrieve the lost package of bug snacks and holds it up, examining the things moving around inside. He's amazed that such a thing even exists.

"Well I'll be damned…" Bill says to the candy spiders.

"There used to be these little living gummy people that we used to give the kids called goombies. They are alive just like the spiders, but were slightly intelligent. They could wave to the children and dance around a little. The kids loved them."

"Sounds kind of horrifying if you ask me," Bill says.

"Yeah, a little bit," Hanks tells him. "They had to take 'em off the market though. Turns out that even though they could dance and wave, all the little gummy people ever wanted to do was masturbate. They'd just masturbate all day and night or hump each other in the bag. The kids still liked them but obviously, their parents didn't want them eating anything that was partaking in vulgar activities."

"I suppose not…" Bill says, wondering what in the world that candy would have been like.

"The company had to switch to selling them to sex shops. There's even goombie porn movies online. Go to pornhub and see for yourself. Search for goombies. It's just gummy candies having sex with themselves or each other. Sometimes a cam girl will put a few of 'em up her butt and wiggle around in front of the camera. It's crazy stuff. You should look it up."

Bill backs away a little. "Nah, I think I'm good. I'm not that adventurous."

Hank laughs and nods his head a little. Then he points at the monitor. "Well, you better get a move on. The kids look like they're getting prickly."

Bill looks over to the screens and sees their little glass bodies twitching and shuffling in their beds. They look like they're about to throw tantrums if they don't get their mid-morning snacks soon. Bill hurries back to the snack cabinet and picks up the pace.

Bill rolls a cart full of dozens of boxes of snacks down the hallway and heads for the first room. He forgot that Hank recommended he do room 218 first, the room with the problem kids. But he's already opening the door to room 220 and thinks it would be rude to turn back now. The room looks like a cross between a hospital room and a padded cell. The walls are colored like Easter eggs, with stripes and polka dots and pictures of little teddy bears, all pastel colors. There are two pillowy beds and a large television on the wall playing cartoons.

Lying in the beds are two glass children. They are so engaged in the show they are watching that they ignore Bill as he walks in with the snacks. He pulls up the cart to the first child to display the goods, but the kid doesn't look his way. It's a young boy with large glass eyes and shaggy crystal hair. Bill has never been so close to a glass child before. They look unreal to him. They don't even look like they're alive. He would have assumed they were crystal sculptures if they weren't breathing and moving. The gases shift and swirl inside the boy's torso. Bright colors curling and fading into each other. It's almost like there's a firework show going on in the child's abdomen.

Bill clears his throat, but the boy doesn't respond. As he makes this noise, a gentle chime rings out in the room. Then he tries coughing to get the kid's attention and the chime rings two more times. Once he lets out a loud sigh and hears another chime, Bill realizes that it must be Hank in the monitoring station signaling to him to not make such disturbing noises around the children. Bill nods to the camera and decides to speak to the boy.

"Um, so…" Bill says. "I've got your snack for you. What would you like?"

Although the kid doesn't respond, the chime rings five times in a row. Bill looks at the camera and holds out his arms. He's about to go back to the monitoring station to ask the old guy what he's supposed to do. But before he leaves, the boy says, "Bug snacks."

It's the only snack Bill knows the name of, so he's happy with the kid's order. He pulls a package of candy spiders from the cart and hands it to the child. The kid doesn't take it. The chime rings again and again with every move Bill makes.

After holding it there for a moment, the kid looks up at Bill with his haunting translucent eyes and says, "What are you an idiot? You have to open it for me."

The way the kid spoke to him in such a bratty way gives Bill the urge to slap him across the face. But he just grumbles to himself and says, "Yes, Your Highness."

He clutches the bag, trying to open it. "Do you want me to feed them to you as well?"

Bill knows that he's being rude and will likely get in

trouble for talking to the kid like this, but he just can't help himself. He really can't stand bratty kids.

Although the chime keeps ringing, the kid doesn't take it as an attack at all, as though being asked to be fed is a pretty normal thing in this place.

The boy responds, "Nah, I'm good."

When Bill tears open the bag, the spiders explode out of the package. They fly all over the child's bed and chest, twitching and squirming through the air.

Bill thinks he's about to have a heart attack for spilling the candy everywhere, like it's going to cause the kid to fly off into a tantrum. But the boy is unfazed by his mess up. He just opens his mouth and all the candy spiders crawl up his body through his glass lips. The kid chews only a little before swallowing.

Bill can see the spiders dissolve within the gases in the child's abdomen. He's never seen a glass child eat anything before, but he knows that they have much different digestive systems than flesh and blood people do. They dissolve their food into gases that are eventually excreted out of their mouths in the form of burps. They don't need to urinate because they don't require much fluid in their diet. Sodium and nitrogen and sugar are far more important to their diet than fruits or vegetables or protein or fiber. They have completely different physiologies that still perplexes scientists to this day. Bill doesn't understand how a human can give birth to something so alien.

When the kid finishes the spiders crawling on his bed, Bill pours the rest of the package on top of him and lets the living candy do the rest. Once he's all done, he takes his snack cart to the kid in the next bed and does it all over again.

Before Bill goes to the next room, he decides to stop by the monitoring station to ask Hank what the hell was up with him ringing a bell at him the whole time. He's not even sure if it was Hank doing it. For all he knew, it could have just been a normal thing that happens in this place. But if it was a warning to Bill that he was doing something wrong, he better find out exactly what the problem was before he enters another room.

He enters the monitoring station and says, "Hey Hank, what was that noise that I kept hearing when—"

Before he can finish, Bill sees the old guy's face in a panic. Hank is jumping up and down, waving his hands around in a frenzy.

"Get to room 218!" Hank yells. "It's an emergency! The kids are going nuts in there."

Bill just gasps and turns his cart around. Then he rushes to the room and bursts through the door. Inside, two glass children are shrieking at the tops of their lungs. Their cries sound like someone is playing a glass harmonica or rubbing their finger along the side of a wine glass. They are the twins that Hank was talking about, Tony and Toni. They look much different from the children in the last room. Their glass bodies are covered in fractures from head to toe and look to have been filled in with some kind of acrylic sealant. The parts of their bodies that are not covered in cracks are all scratched up and blurry. He can barely make out the colorful gases within their abdomens. Because they are twins, Bill wonders if the scratches were caused by them rubbing together in the womb before they were even born. He imagines that the survival of twin glass fetuses is probably pretty rare.

"Sorry I'm late," Bill tells them, rolling the cart toward the closest child. "I have your snacks right here."

But he soon realizes that the kids aren't upset by his tardiness. Something else is wrong with them. The two children are pointing at each other and screaming.

"What's wrong?" Bill asks.

"Toni won't stop looking at me!" the boy yells, pointing at his sister.

"No, Tony won't stop looking at *me!*" the girl cries, pointing at her brother.

"Stop looking at me!" Tony cries.

"Stop looking at *me!*" Toni yells.

Bill doesn't know how to deal with whiny children. He just stands there, confused about what he's supposed to do. He wonders if he shouldn't go get Linda and have her deal with it. But he can tell by the gases swirling chaotically around inside the glass children, it's not going to be long before they start to crack.

He wheels the cart to the middle of the room and stands between the two beds, blocking them from each other's line of sight. The children stop screaming.

"There," Bill tells them. "Now neither of you can see the other."

The children calm themselves, breathing rapidly.

"I brought snacks for you both of you," Bill says. "What would you like?"

"I don't want anything," Tony says, turning away in a huff.

Bill turns to his sister. "What about you? Do you want a snack?"

The girl pouts and fumes. The gases in her body pulse with her breaths. After she regains herself, she says, "Give me some puff puffs, some wiggle wonkers, two boxes of jimmy jams, and a doo log."

Bill lets out a sigh and looks at the snacks. He has no idea what any of them are without his glasses, so he picks them up one at a time and tries to read the text. The logos of the products are so stylized that they might as well be written in Japanese.

Toni starts pointing them out with her splintered fingers. "That one. That one. That one. Those two. And that one."

Bill tries to remember the ones she picked out and grabs the one closest. He begins cracking open the box, but it causes Toni's eyes to widen and her gases to spin.

"No, I want to do it!" she cries, holding out her hands.

Bill goes to hand her the box, but she shakes her head and pushes it away as hard as she can with her minuscule amount of strength.

"You already opened it," she says. "I want a new one."

He hands her a new box, but she's not able to hold it upright and it falls on the bed next to her. She ignores it and points at another snack.

"Okay…" Bill says, trying to keep as soft a tone as possible.

He gives her the snack and she is able to hold it for quite a bit longer than the last one before it falls. He hands them off one at a time until the snacks are piled up on her bed. Then she looks at them all with pride and a smile forms on her face. Her glass pigtails rattle against her shoulders.

"I can open them myself," Toni says, trying to lift the lightest package in her tiny hands. "I've been practicing."

She struggles with it for several minutes but can't get it open. Bill tries to go in to help her but she just cries out and he backs off. He decides to leave her be.

Assuming he's finished, Bill returns to his cart and pushes it toward the exit. But then the boy gets upset and yells, "Hey! What about me?"

Bill looks back at him. "You said you didn't want anything."

The boy ignores his words and cries, "You gave Toni all those snacks and gave nothing to me!"

Bill fights back the urge to argue and turns the cart around. "What would you like?"

"Give me everything you gave to Toni," he says.

Bill shrugs. "Okay, fine."

He hands Tony a box of wiggle wonkers and Tony freaks out and pushes the box away. "Ewww! I hate those!"

"You said you wanted everything I gave to your sister," Bill says.

"They're so gross!" Tony says. Then he points out different products. "Give me those, those, those, and those."

None of the choices are the same as Toni's, but Bill hands them over anyway. Once he stacks them up on the bed, Bill turns to leave, but Tony isn't done with him.

"I can't open these!" the boy cries.

Bill turns back. "Your sister can open them."

"No, she can't," he argues. "She's just faking. Nobody can open them."

Bill lets out a sigh and opens the packages one at a time, then hands their contents to the boy. When he gets the snack that is shaped like a sponge, he squeezes it in his mouth and sugary pink liquid drains down his chin and neck.

"Is that everything you need?" Bill asks.

Tony nods.

Then Toni says, "Open mine too! You opened Tony's but not mine!"

Bill doesn't argue. He returns to the girl's bed and opens all of her snacks for her. Because she can't hold it on her own, he has to feed her the doo log. It looks kind of like a salt-and-chocolate-covered pretzel stick but is as soft as a Twinkie. Bill wonders why in the world they'd name something so clearly poop-shaped would be labeled a doo-log. It's almost as though snack companies are trolling children of the new generation.

As Bill feeds the girl, the boy says, "I want to watch a movie!"

The kid says this in such a demanding voice that Bill can tell he's not willing to wait until his sister's done eating her doo log.

Bill has to try to buy a little time, so he asks the kid,

"What kind of movie do you want to watch?"

The boy says, "I want to watch the best movie in the world."

Bill snickers at his response. "Well, the best movie in the world is Apocalypse Now, but I doubt they'd let you watch something like that."

"Why not?" Tony asks. "I'm fifteen. I can watch anything I want."

"You're not fifteen!" Toni cries, spitting out salty chocolate. "You're the same age as me!"

"I'm going to be fifteen in eight months so I'm practically an adult. I want to watch Apocalypse Now."

Bill realizes he made a mistake. He knows that glass children are not able to watch war movies. In fact, they can't watch almost any movie that's been made before they were born. They have to watch movies made specifically for them. Because they can't experience anything too stressful or anything that might rile their emotions, movies are now made without any kind of conflict whatsoever. They almost always feature a person who gets everything they want whenever they want without struggle or hard work. Like a movie about a musician who wants to hit it big and will get everything handed to them immediately without ever having to try. Everyone is nice and happy in movies. Characters never face challenges. They never get hurt or disappointed. They never lose at anything. And because of this, most movies are incredibly boring. Even glass children aren't engaged by them. Bill wonders why they even get made.

When Toni finishes eating, Bill gets up and goes to

the television. He picks up the remote and puts on the kids' movie channel. There's a cartoon playing about two talking cats sitting in a living room.

"I don't want to watch that," Toni says. "It's offensive."

Bill is confused. "How is it offensive?"

"It's abusive to animals," Toni says.

"They're not real animals," Bill explains. "They're just cartoons."

"But they've been left home all alone," Toni says. "They're being psychologically scarred by their owners. It's animal abuse."

Bill shrugs and puts on another movie. This one is a lot older and is about a bunch of kids at a birthday party opening presents and having fun.

"I can't believe you support movies like this!" Toni says.

"What's wrong with it?" Bill asks.

Toni explains, "None of the kids are made out of glass. I don't want to watch anything without glass actors."

Bill is beginning to lose patience. "Are there *any* movies with glass actors? I didn't think they were able to act."

"Of course they can act!" Toni yells. "Glass children are the best actors in the world!"

"But isn't that dangerous?" he asks. "They could break."

"Put on a movie with glass children in it!" Toni cries.

Bill struggles with the remote, trying to find something with glass children.

"I want to watch Apocalypse Now," Tony says. "There's only glass children in Apocalypse Now."

Bill snickers when the kid says this, imagining a version of Apocalypse Now with only glass actors.

"Apocalypse Now sounds boring," Toni says.

"You haven't even seen it!" Tony says.

"Neither have you!" Toni says.

Bill lets out a sigh. He can't handle spending this much time with these kids.

"There aren't any glass children in Apocalypse Now," Bill says. "It's an old man movie. Neither of you would like it."

"Yeah, it's an old man movie!" Toni yells at her brother.

"It is not!" Tony yells at his sister.

"I'll tell you what," Bill says. "I'm going to think of a number between one to ten. Whoever guesses closest gets to choose the movie."

"Seven," Tony says.

Toni cries, "No fair! I was going to guess seven!"

"It's not seven," Bill says to shut them up.

"Then I guess three," Tony says.

"I'm guessing four," Toni says.

Bill points to the girl. "It's five, so you win. What do you want to watch?"

The girl's face lights up with excitement. "Anything that's not Apocalypse Now."

"No fair!" Tony cries.

The girl bounces in triumph. The colors in her chest swirl around with glee. "I won! I won!"

Bill shrugs and tosses on a random kids' movie.

"Easy enough," he says.

Then he races out of the room before they change their mind and want him to put on something else.

Bill hands out snacks to the rest of the kids in the rooms, each one worse than the last, though none of them were quite as picky or took as much time as the twins. He puts the cart away and goes back to the monitoring station.

"God damn those kids are a pain in the ass," Bill tells Hank, ready to punch his fist through one of the monitors.

Hank just laughs at him.

"I need a smoke," Bill says. "And some whiskey. A hell of a lot of whiskey."

Hank sighs. "Tell me about it. They outlawed alcohol because they don't want parents drinking around their kids, but with the world the way it is now we need liquor more than ever."

"I got a few bottles at home," Bill says. "Stashed 'em away before they took 'em all off the shelves. I was planning on saving them for a special occasion but when I get home I don't think I'll be able to resist cracking one open."

Hank nods. "Not a bad idea. If you can smuggle a flask in tomorrow give me little."

Bill laughs. "Are you shitting me? I don't got none to spare."

"I'll turn you in if you don't," Hank says, giving him a dirty look.

"And I'll let them know you don't need that wheelchair," Bill says.

They glare at each other for a moment and then just chuckle.

"I'll tell you what," Bill says. "After we clock out, if you want to swing by my place we can have a couple shots together. I don't like to drink alone anyway."

"Sounds good to me," Hank says. Then they fist bump each other.

Bill and Hank sit around chatting for a while. Even though they're almost twenty years apart, the two seem to have a lot in common. They mostly bond over what they have to complain about. Both of them are depressed over not being able to bowl anymore. They both miss pubs and hunting and going to ball games. They both find comfort in complaining about what the world's come to.

After a while, Hank looks at his checklist next to him and says, "Hey, it looks like you missed one. The girl in room 219. She didn't get her snack."

"You sure?" Bill asks. "I thought I got them all."

"Yeah, you definitely missed her. I can see the contents of their stomachs from the monitors and she's not eaten anything yet."

"Damn," Bill says, scratching his head. "Sorry about that."

Hank shakes his head. "Don't worry about it. Most people miss her. It's probably because she doesn't call attention to herself or make a fuss. Kind of a sweet kid. But something about that girl's different from the others. She's one of the first glass kids born in this city. Not many around that's her age. She's an odd one."

"Odd?" Bill asks. "How?"

Hank nods toward the monitor. "Go in there and see for yourself. You'll like her, but she'll haunt your dreams."

"What's that supposed to mean?" Bill asks, but Hank just waves him in the direction of the exit.

Bill doesn't know how to take that information. He gets a little nervous.

Before Bill is able to pry further, Hank says, "She likes the stuff in the green box. Bring her some of that."

Bill nods his head and returns to the snack cupboard, wondering what the hell the old man is on about. *All* the glass children are odd as far as he's concerned. He can't imagine she'd be any stranger than the others he's met.

CHAPTER
THREE

Carrying boxes of green snacks, Bill enters Room 219. It is completely silent. There's nothing playing on the television. It doesn't look like it's been turned on in months. A young girl lies alone in the bed, with her fingers crossed and a distant gaze. She glistens more than the other glass children, like her hard exterior has been shined and cleaned with Windex. Her hair is molded in a bob-styled haircut as though she was born with this particular hairstyle. She's like a perfect glass figurine but for a small crack down the center of her forehead.

When she looks up at Bill, a relaxed smile appears on her face.

"Hello," she says. "You're new. Are you Gwendolyn's replacement?"

Bill stands there a little confused. He says, "I guess so. It's my first day."

"It's a shame what happened to her," the girl says. "She was really nice."

"I'm sure she was," Bill says, even though he has no idea who she's talking about.

"What's your name?" the girl asks.

"My name's Bill," he says. "But people call me Big Bill, from the car commercials."

The girl smiles wider. "Hello, Big Bill. My name is Madeline, but people call me Maddie."

Bill nods. "Hi there, Maddie. It's good to meet you."

Although he normally doesn't feel comfortable around children, he likes this girl's demeanor. He understands why Hank said that he'd like her. She's not an annoying selfish brat like the others. She's actually rather polite.

"Come sit with me," Maddie tells him. "I'm rather lonely in here."

Bill nods and goes to her. "I see you have the room to yourself. What happened to your roommate?"

He gestures to the empty bed next to her as he takes a seat in the chair by her bed.

"She popped," Maddie says. "My roommates always pop eventually."

The way she says this in a matter-of-fact tone sends a shiver down Bill's spine.

"So Hank says you like this green stuff," Bill says, holding up the boxed snacks. "I brought you plenty."

Upon closer inspection, he observes how this girl is much different from the others. The gases in her body are unique. More like liquids than gas, they undulate within her glass abdomen like a lava lamp. He wonders if it's because she's older than the others or maybe because she's some kind of mutant among the glass generation. Either way, Bill agrees with Hank when he said there's something odd about this one.

"Can you feed it to me?" Maddie asks. "I don't need you to, but it will give us a chance to chat. They won't get mad at you if I request some of your time."

The way she asks this creeps Bill right out. He had to feed other glass children today, but none of them did it because they wanted to spend time with him. Very few people apart from his drinking buddies have ever desired to spend their time with him. But he assumes that this girl must be so lonely that anyone, even Bill, would be preferable to being alone.

"Sure," Bill says. "I don't mind."

He opens up the boxes and pulls out a handful of candy. It looks like wheatgrass but it feels more like a bunch of toothpicks made of quartz. He holds it toward her open mouth and she bites into the green candy, causing it to shatter and crumble down her chin.

"It tastes different than when Gwendolyn fed me," Maddie says. "Your sweat has a more hearty flavor than hers did."

Bill's eyes widen when she says this. He wipes his hands on his overalls. "Oh, I'm so sorry. I didn't realize I was sweating on your food."

The girl smiles. "You don't need to apologize. I like the taste of human sweat. Its saltiness is more pleasing than the sodium that's added to our normal food."

Bill shifts his weight anxiously. He was embarrassed by adding sweat to her food, but having her enjoy it is downright concerning. If she wasn't a kid he'd think it was borderline perverse.

Despite his awkwardness, Bill takes another pinch

CARLTON MELLICK III

of grass crystals from the package and feeds it to the girl, hoping his hands aren't as sweaty as they were before. But as he holds it toward her mouth, she sucks his fingers between her lips and drinks the fluids from his flesh. He can feel her hard lips against his knuckles and the texture of her dull teeth scraping against his skin. Bill gets so unnerved by this that he drops the candy on her glossy tongue and pulls his hand away.

Bill stands up and rubs his hands on his pants. "Okay, this is getting inappropriate. I draw the line at having my fingers in your mouth."

"I'm sorry," Maddie says, a genuine look of concern on her face. "I didn't mean to make you uncomfortable. I just crave salt and the food here doesn't contain enough of it."

Bill shakes off the awkwardness and says, "I'll get you all the salt you want. Just don't go licking my fingers like that. It's not normal."

Maddie nods her glass head and gestures for him to sit back down. "I won't do it again if it makes you uncomfortable. My last attendant didn't mind so much, but she was a woman. I supposed an older man like yourself can't help but see it as inappropriate, maybe even sexual. But I promise that if I lick your fingers I don't mean it in that way whatsoever."

Bill only gets more unsettled by her response. He doesn't know what to say to the girl. Unlike the other glass children who all seemed immature for their age, this girl's the complete opposite. She speaks as though she's wise beyond even his level of understanding. He

48

kind of wants to just walk out of the room and never come back.

"Don't leave," Maddie says, as though she was reading his mind. "You can hand me the food and I will eat it myself. I just enjoy the company."

Bill agrees but he stays on guard. He hands her another pinch of the grass-like candy and she takes it in her soft fragile hands, then sucks on them like tiny candy canes.

"You've never been married," Maddie says to him. "Isn't it lonely living all by yourself for so long?"

Bill is confused by her line of questioning. "How do you know I've never been married?"

Maddie smiles and sinks into her pillow. "I'm sure it's nice living your life by your own rules, but not having anyone to share it with just sounds sad to me. Every accomplishment you make must be bittersweet. Every time you sold a car for more than it was worth or every time you expanded to a new location, it must have been disappointing not having somebody who could be happy for you and celebrate all your victories by your side. Even if you enjoy having all of your personal freedoms, in the end, you only feel alone and empty at the end of the day. It's kind of tragic in my opinion."

Bill's expression becomes one of shock. He can't imagine how the little girl knows about his personal life or his innermost thoughts. She's not at all wrong, and that only makes it all the more frightening to him.

Bill doesn't know what else to say but, "How in the hell do you know all of this about me?" He doesn't even realize that he's swearing in a child's presence.

"I can see it in you," the girl says. "Like you can see my whole spirit inside of my glass body, I can see yours through your sad glossy eyes. You regret a lot about your life. In fact, your regrets have made you who you are. It's too bad you never trusted another person enough to let them into your life. It's too bad that you were never able to fully embrace the life you always truly wanted."

When she finishes speaking, Bill can't help but get upset. He doesn't know if she's a witch or a mind reader, but her words have struck a nerve and provoked a surge of anger within him.

"Look," Bill yells. "I don't know who or what you think you are, but I didn't come here to have some little shit talk down to me about how I messed up my life. I was perfectly happy with everything until you glass brats came along and fucked everything up. My house, my car, even my fucking retirement, I had to give them all up to support you freakish monstrosities of nature. Big Bill Mason is not the pathetic lonely loser you think I am. I love who I am. I don't need anyone else. I'm perfectly happy being me."

"I'm sorry, Big Bill," Maddie says. "I didn't mean to upset you."

Bill tosses the rest of the snacks on the girl's bed and says, "Feed yourself if you're so smart. I don't have time for this bullshit."

Then he storms out of the room and heads for the bathroom, trying to pull the pink jumpsuit off of his body. He doesn't care if he gets fired. He doesn't care if he goes to jail. He just doesn't want to spend one more second with any of these weird kids for the rest of his life.

Bill hangs out in the bathroom for a good half hour, staring at himself in the mirror, taking a big dump, washing his hands at least a dozen times, before Hank wheels himself inside to check in on him.

"Don't let it get to you," Hank tells him. "I said the girl was odd. She freaks out everyone on their first day."

Bill looks at the old guy in the wheelchair and steps toward him. "What the hell was she on about? How'd she know about my car business? How'd she know I was never married?"

Hank shrugs. "She's an observant type. She picks up on those kinds of things."

"She's a fucking freak," Bill says.

Hank snickers at his words. "Yeah, they're all freaks. The kids are made out of glass for Christ's sake. But Maddie's a good one. She wasn't raised like the others. She wasn't spoiled rotten or raised like a fragile little flower. As one of the first kids born of glass, her parents thought she was some kind of hellspawn and kept her locked in their basement. It's a miracle she even survived. But what didn't kill her made her stronger. Out of all the kids on our block, she's the only one that gives me hope for the future."

Bill lets out a sigh and puts his head in the sink, letting water roll over his face.

"I know it's bullshit that you were forced to do this job against your will," Hank continues, "but these kids need you. Maddie needs you. Don't let them get under your skin. I was just like you when I first started, but I've come to understand that what we do here is important. I'm actually happy that I'm doing what I can for the future generation. It's better than just rotting away in some home somewhere. It's worth all the bullshit we have to put up with."

Bill rubs water in what remains of his hair and then shakes it across his pink uniform. Then he looks at Hank. "Says the guy pretending to be in a wheelchair."

Hank just laughs at him. He wheels himself backward toward the bathroom exit. "Go ahead and feel sorry for yourself in here for as long as you want, but I'm going back to my post. Come see me once you calm down. No matter how shitty they might act, those kids need you." He pushes open the door and says, "I hope you don't give up and call it quits like all the others."

When Hank is gone, Bill just feels even more worked up. He wants to give up and leave, but he can't get himself to go. Maybe it's the threat of jail time or the words the old guy told to him, but he doesn't think it's right to just leave. No matter how much he hates those kids, he knows that he'd hate himself even more if he just walked out on them. Big Bill Mason is a lot of things, but he's no coward. He's no quitter.

It only takes a few more minutes before Bill composes himself and returns to his duties. He has to go from room to room, fluffing pillows and changing movies and listening to all the children's annoying requests, but Bill soldiers through. The kids are even more annoying than the first time he had to interact with them, but he tries not to let their spoiled nature get to him. He knows they have it even worse than he does. Even though he has to do a job without pay, at least he's not stuck in bed during the most lively time of his life. When he was their age, he was able to date girls and play ball with his friends and drink liquor stashed in his daddy's garage when his parents were out of town. He was able to live life to the fullest as a teenager, but these kids will never be able to experience what he was able to. Even once they become adults, they're still going to be stuck as invalids and have others taking care of them. If he were in their situation during any time of his life he would have rather been dead. The least he can offer is a little of his time to give them some kind of semblance of happiness, even if they are a bunch of little shits.

But even as he grows comfortable dealing with the annoying ones, Bill's still nervous about interacting with Maddie. If she's going to reach into his soul and pull out all the delicate, vulnerable parts then he'd rather avoid her altogether. But it isn't long before he's got no choice but to check in on the girl. He's not allowed to go more than an hour without checking in on each of the glass children and it's been well over that with Maddie. With all the other annoying snots taken care of, he doesn't have any excuse not to check in on her. Even Hank won't let him off the hook until he finally attends to the girl.

As Bill enters Maddie's room, the girl is propped up in her bed with her hands crossed. She doesn't seem to have moved much since his last visit. She hasn't touched the snacks that remain on the side of her bed. She's just staring forward as though engaged in a very exciting movie despite the fact that the television isn't on.

"You're back," Maddie says, not looking at him. "I'm sorry I scared you off before."

Bill chuckles nervously. "You didn't scare me off. Big Bill Mason doesn't scare so easily."

There's a moment of silence. The girl doesn't respond to his comment, but even he doesn't believe his words to be true. He breaks the silence by saying, "I was just coming in to see if you needed anything."

"I mostly just need some company," Maddie says. Then she looks over at him. "But I'll take those salt packets you have in your pocket."

Her words terrify Bill, but he tries to keep a strong composure.

He pulls the salt packets out of the pockets in his jumpsuit and says, "Nothing gets past you, I guess. I got these from the cafeteria, figuring you might want them."

Bill sits down and tears one of them open, then hands it to her. She takes it and pours the salt down her throat.

After she guzzles down three packets, Maddie says, "The food they give us is designed for young children.

54

They haven't yet learned how important salt is to teenagers. We can't grow without it."

Bill opens another pack of salt and gives it to her. The girl takes it into her glass fingers and sucks the salt out.

"People have the wrong idea about us," Maddie says. "We're not as fragile as everyone thinks. Far less fragile than the generations who came before us."

Bill wonders if she's just being a pretentious teenager. Obviously what she's saying is untrue. There's no one more fragile than the glass children.

"Just because we're made of glass doesn't make us weak," the girl says. "We are actually stronger than you. If the environment fails, if the sun dies, if crops can no longer grow, we'll still be able to live. They say the reason we were born was some mistake, but we are a natural evolution of the human species. We were made to withstand environmental collapse."

Bill doesn't know whether to be afraid or laugh at her statement. He decides not to take her too seriously.

"I don't know about that," he says. "Maybe you're a little too deep for me."

But the girl doesn't let it go. "If people raised us the right way we would be thriving. They think because we're glass that they must pad the world for us, make it so that we don't break. But it's unnecessary. If we were taught instead to deal with the dangers of the world we would grow much sturdier. A strong wind will blow us over and cause us to crack, but not if we walk into the wind. Falling on concrete will break us into pieces, but not if we learn proper balance. Keeping us in beds isn't going to protect us. It's just going to make it harder for us in the long run. But it's what makes people of your generation feel better about themselves." The girl places her delicate glass hand on Bill's knee. "Not you, of course. As someone who's never had children, you don't have the urge to do whatever it takes to protect us. But we could use more people like you, who think we should just deal with the harshness of the world than trying to shelter us from it. We are glass but we are what the world needs to make itself stronger. Without us, the human race would not survive."

Bill stares forward, inching away from the girl's hand on his knee. He's caught off guard by the girl's words, but he's not entirely turned off by them. She's saying exactly the same thoughts that he's been thinking. He's surprised that a kid her age agrees that the younger generation is worse off by being treated in the delicate way they are.

Bill decides this girl is mature enough to speak to her like a normal person. He says, "You got a good head on your shoulders, girl." A smile grows on his face. "When I was a boy, I was not treated gingerly whatsoever. I was beaten into the man I am now. Nobody sheltered me from the harshness of the world. I had to fight my way up, become strong in order to survive. If the kids these days weren't treated so delicately they would learn character. They'd grow some backbone and know how to take care of themselves."

The girl shakes her head. "I don't think your upbringing made you strong. It made you weak. Perhaps you have a tough exterior, but inside you are as fragile as my glass skin. Love makes a man strong inside. You've never been loved enough to gain that strength. What people don't understand about glass children is that we are born with love swirling inside of us." The girl points at her abdomen. "We don't need any emotional support in order to be strong. Those of your generation focus so much on the weak exterior of our bodies that you don't realize how strong we are inside. We don't bleed to death, we don't have organ failure, we cannot get cancer, we can breathe without oxygen, we can survive with a minimal amount of food that can be produced without damaging the environment. And on top of that, not a single child of our generation has ever been so emotionally damaged that we've been compelled to commit suicide. We have strong hearts. Our emotions will never kill us."

Bill thinks about her words for a moment. He likes what she's saying, but he doesn't believe it. He thinks she's got to be over-exaggerating the strengths of her fragile generation.

Before he realizes what he's doing, Bill argues, "But you shatter whenever you get stressed out. How is that strong? Your emotions kill your people all the time. Glass children break. They pop, just like your past roommates. That's not something that my generation ever did."

Bill feels bad for arguing with a child, but she doesn't seem fazed by his words. She just calmly shakes her head.

"When you're raised without any understanding of stress, of course you're going to pop," Maddie says. "Stress wouldn't be an issue if we weren't sheltered from it. But we aren't affected by the long-term effects of stress like your generation is. Even the most spoiled child in this daycare center will get stronger with every stressful situation they survive. It doesn't linger in them. It doesn't give them PTSD. No matter what happens to them, they never want to die. Being trapped in our beds all day every day might make us bored, but it never makes us want to end our lives. Could you say the same?"

Bill thinks about it for a moment. He did feel sorry for the children, no matter how bratty they all were. But he would never be able to trade places with them. He'd rather be dead than spend the rest of his life in a hospital bed.

"I guess you got a point," Bill says. "You kids have to deal with a lot more than I had to when I was your age. I don't think I could deal with it the same way you do."

The girl nods. "If you want to help the other children that are in your care, you shouldn't just give them what they want. You should introduce stress into their lives in small doses, as much as you can. Not enough to kill them, of course. Just tell them *no* every once in a while. I know it's against the rules and exactly the opposite of what you've been asked to do. But if you have any concern for the futures of those in your care, you should help them grow strong."

Bill can't believe what the girl's talking about. He just shrugs a little and says, "I don't know. I don't want to mess things up. I'm not any good with kids."

Maddie stares through him with her glossy glass eyeballs. "Don't be afraid. Even if they hate you for it, you'll help them in the long run. Our generation shouldn't be locked away in a facility for the rest of our lives. We will inherit the world one day, and we won't be able to do it if your generation only sees us as fragile little glass ornaments. The world has to understand that we're strong and will make things better if only we're given the chance. If you're too worried that we'll break then that's exactly what we'll eventually do."

Bill doesn't know what to say. The girl is talking like someone at least twice her age. Hell, it's almost like she's saying something that he'd say himself if only he had any kind of optimism for the younger generations. He always thought they didn't stand a chance to survive in the harsh world the way they are now, but maybe what the kid is saying has a little bit of truth. Even though they're made of glass, maybe these children do have some kind of strength that Bill never considered before. He wonders if there really is something he can do to help them grow stronger and not be such spoiled little annoying brats for the rest of their lives.

Once the girl is done preaching about the strengths and weaknesses of being part of the glass children generation, they start chatting about other things that are not so deep and serious. He realizes he's able to have a normal conversation with one of these young kids without having to walk on eggshells around her. They talk about cars and fishing and all the things that Bill holds dear.

After spending some time with Maddie, Bill starts to feel a connection to the girl. At first he doesn't know why, but then he realizes it's because she reminds him of somebody he used to know a long time ago. Maddie is a lot like how he remembered his little sister, Jane. She was a lot like Maddie. Smart as a whip. Confident and relaxed no matter who she was around. She was much younger than him yet somehow talked down to him like he was some kind of simpleton. Jane was a great kid that Bill loved dearly. But she died of a tumor in her bladder when she was in her first year of high school because their shithead father was too broke to take her to the hospital once she first started showing signs of pain and swelling in her abdomen.

Bill misses his little sister more than anything. He always thought she was the best of them. Far better than he was at almost everything when they were young. She was a braver and more confident woman than their old ma, and far kinder a soul than their old man. If only she lived Bill knows that he would have been a better person in his old age. She was the only shining light in the deep filthy pit of an existence Bill was raised within. She never should have been taken away so young, with her whole life ahead of her. Bill wonders what it would've been like if his sister was one of these children made of glass. It would've broken his heart to see her stuck in a bed or forced to live in a padded world of pillows and rubber walkways, but if she was made of glass she wouldn't have died of some tumor. With her heart as strong as it was, nothing would've stopped her as long as her glass shell stayed intact. But she wasn't born into the right family. She wasn't born in the right era. And nothing's going to bring her back.

As Bill sits and talks with the glass girl, he imagines

that it's his little sister he's spending time with. He never got a chance to say goodbye to her. She died while he was at school, all alone in incredible agony. But, for a moment, he's able to pretend that the conversation he's having with Maddie is the same one he would have had with his sister while she was in the hospital. Just before the end.

By the time he leaves the room, Bill's wiping tears from his eyes. He says nothing's wrong, but the glass girl seems to know everything that's going on in that thick skull of his.

She says, "I'm sorry for your loss."

And Bill just nods his head, saying, "Let me know if you need anything."

But before she can respond, Bill's out in the hallway and heading back toward the snack room to cry. He was always taught that grown men don't cry, but all the people who ever told him that are long dead. So he just lets it all out, right in the middle of the hallway for everyone to see. He hides away in the snack room and lets the rest of it out. It doesn't last long. When his emotions settle, he wipes the tears from his face and composes himself. He doesn't want to embarrass himself, even to one of the glass children. So he gets over it, quickly and abruptly, just as he's gotten over every hard emotion that's ever broken his heart in two.

When Bill goes back to the monitoring station, he realizes that Hank was watching and listening to everything that went on in the room with Maddie. The old guy just looks up at Bill and gives him a nod.

"Sweet girl, isn't she?" Hank asks.

Bill just nods and says, "Yeah, she's an angel."

"A bit of a mindfuck though, right?"

Bill nods again. "Yeah. How the hell is she the same age as the others?"

"She's special," Hank says. "Best of the bunch."

Bill agrees. "Too bad they're all not as bright as her."

Hank looks over at him. "They're all pretty bright once you get to know them. If they weren't spoiled so much maybe people would realize it. I've been watching these kids long enough to know there's more to them than meets the eye. Like the girl said, they're not as delicate as they seem."

"Not you, too," Bill says.

Hank shrugs. "I just say it as I see it."

Without being told, Bill sees another kid getting worked up on one of the monitors and rushes out of the room to see what the fuss is about.

CHAPTER
FOUR

Bill goes to room 218 where the twins are having another fight. When he goes inside, Bill sees that they are caught up in another pointless argument with each other.

"What's the problem, kids?" Bill asks with a forced smile on his face, trying to be as pleasant as he can be even though he knows that his smile is probably more terrifying than it is pleasing. Luckily, the kids don't even look in his direction or notice the awkward smile on his face.

"Toni thinks she's prettier than I am," Tony says.

"I *am* prettier!" Toni cries.

"No, you're not! You have more cracks in your face than I do. Of course I'm prettier."

"But I'm a girl! Girls are always prettier than boys!"

"Boys can be pretty too!" Tony says.

"Not as pretty as girls."

"Boys are way prettier than girls."

"No, they're not!"

"They are if the girl has as many cracks in their face as you do."

"I'm still pretty even with cracks in my face. Gwendolyn told me so!"

Tony looks over at Bill and says, "Tell this busted-up skank that I'm prettier than she is."

Toni looks over at Bill and says, "Tell my stupid brother that boys can't be prettier than girls."

They stare at Bill for a while, but the old guy doesn't know what to say. To him, neither of them is pretty at all. They are both cracked and scraped up and are made of glass. He can't see them as anything but freaks. But he knows that he can't tell them that one is prettier than the other without getting himself into trouble. He has to just lie to them.

"I think you're both equally pretty," he tells them.

Saying the words causes him to die a little inside, but he doesn't think there's any other response he could give. Unfortunately, they react as though it was the worst possible thing he could have said. Neither of them is happy with being equally pretty.

"We are not!" Toni cries.

"There's *nothing* pretty about her!" Tony cries. "I'm the only pretty one."

"You're twins," Bill says. "Besides being a boy and a girl, you look practically the same to me."

The children go into an uproar. The gases in their bodies swirl with intensity. The bell chimes in the room, indicating that Bill must be doing something horribly wrong. But there's nothing else Bill can think of to say.

"What!" Toni cries. "No we don't!"

"I don't look anything like this ugly bitch!" Tony yells

Bill holds up his hands. "I'm just saying that you're both pretty. There's no reason to get upset over that."

The bell chimes three more times.

"You really think he's as pretty as I am?" Toni asks. "What's wrong with you?"

"Yeah, are you blind? I'm obviously prettier."

Bill shrugs and says, "Hey, I'm an old man. Compared to me, you're both pretty. What do I know?"

He thinks this will be enough to calm them down, but it only upsets them more. Their insides swirl so quickly that they are nearly about to erupt.

"But look at her!" Tony cries. "She has so many cracks in her face that she looks like a monster!"

"I do not!" Toni cries.

"Yes you do!"

"If we had the same amount of cracks in our faces I'd be way prettier than you are."

"But we don't so I'll always be prettier," Tony says.

"Not if the old guy cracks your face for me," Toni says.

"He wouldn't do that. He's not allowed."

"Yes, he would." Toni points at Bill. "He has to do everything we say. If I tell him to crack your face, then he can't refuse."

"He can't do that!"

Toni looks at Bill and says, "Crack his face for me. Give him as many cracks as I have so that I can prove that I'm prettier."

Tony looks at Bill and says, "You can't crack my face. You'll be fired if you do!"

"He'll be fired if he doesn't!" Toni cries.

Bill just stands there, not sure how to respond. He can't bring harm to any of the children, but he doesn't know how to talk them down. He wonders if he shouldn't just leave and ask someone else for help. Surely he's not the first volunteer to be forced into such a difficult situation.

"I'm not allowed to hurt your brother," he tells Toni. "Besides, why is it so important to be prettier than he is? Beauty is in the eye of the beholder. Some people will think you're prettier than he is. Other people will think he's prettier. Nobody is ever the prettiest to everyone."

"But I'm the prettiest to everyone!" Toni cries.

"No, I'm the prettiest to everyone!" Tony cries.

Their gases shake and quiver, boiling inside their glass cases. The bell chimes over and over again. Bill can't take it anymore. He can't contain his emotions and snaps at them.

"Nobody is prettiest!" Bill cries.

The children go quiet.

"You're made of fucking glass!" Bill yells. "You're not even human. How the fuck can either of you think you're pretty at all? You're both a couple of freaks!"

The kids stare at him with open mouths, shocked that anyone would ever talk to them in such a manner. The gases in their abdomens spin so violently that they become miniature tornadoes in their hollow glass husks. Bill realizes he's made a huge mistake and tries to calm them down.

"I'm sorry, I didn't mean it…"

But it's too late. As the children erupt into high-pitched cries, cracks splinter across their glass frames. Red gases leak from the fissures. Bill can't do anything to prevent it from happening. The children are going to pop.

The door to the room bursts open and Linda races in with three security guards in pink uniforms, carrying a mountain of presents in their arms.

"Surprise!" Linda says in a bright cheerful tone. "Happy spontaneous birthday! Your fifth one this year!"

The second the children see the presents, their emotions relax. The cracks don't grow any larger. As the men in pink pile brightly colored gifts on top of their beds, the kids immediately forget why they were upset in the first place. Their frowns turn to smiles. Their gases change to a joyful blue and pastel purple. The emergency was diverted. The children are saved.

But before Bill can say any kind of apology, Linda whispers to one of the security guards, "Get him the fuck out of here."

Then Bill is forcefully removed from the room.

Back in the monitoring station, Hank can't even look at Bill. He just shakes his head and grunts a couple of times, watching the children on the monitor.

"That was really immature, man," Hank says. "Really immature."

Bill doesn't argue with him. He just lowers his head and says, "God damnit…"

When the twins are all better, their fissures closed with acrylic paste, their presents all opened, and they become busy playing with all of their brand new toys, Linda leaves the room. Her face goes from happy and cheerful to absolutely livid the second she walks out of the door. Then she goes for Bill, charging into the monitoring station as though she's ready to rip his throat out with her bare hands.

"What the hell were you thinking?" Linda yells. "You can't talk to those kids that way."

Bill shakes his head and tries to apologize. "I know. I'm sorry. I just snapped. Kids just do that to me."

Linda gets in his face. "You could have killed them. If Hank didn't sound the alarm in time they would have popped."

"I said I'm sorry, lady." Bill takes a step back. "I warned you, didn't I? I told you I'm no good with kids. It's your fault you didn't listen to me."

"Don't blame this on me. All you had to do was be a little nice to them and they would've been fine. You could have even just kept your mouth shut the whole time. But you had to go and call them ugly."

"I didn't call them ugly. I just said neither of them was the prettiest."

"That's just as bad as calling them ugly!"

"You also called them a couple of freaks," Hank adds.

Bill backpedals. "Hey, one of them was demanding that I crack the other one open. What the hell was I supposed to do in that situation?"

"*Anything* but call them both ugly," Linda says. "I told you that if you were given any impossible tasks to just come get me. We have procedures for handling that kind of thing."

"Like giving them spontaneous birthdays?" Bill asks. "It's no wonder they're so fucking spoiled. They get birthdays whenever they get upset. You're rewarding bad behavior."

"Don't tell me how to do my job."

"If you didn't give them everything they wanted whenever they wanted maybe they wouldn't get so upset all the time. Maybe they'd not crack and pop every time things didn't go their way. You know how many times my own dad called me ugly when I was a kid? That didn't faze me for a second. You pamper kids and they come out soft. They get strong through facing hardship."

Linda just ignores his argument. "If we weren't so short-staffed right now you'd be spending the rest of your life in jail for what you did."

"Wait… So you're not firing me? You mean you still want me to take care of these kids?"

"Hell no. You're not going anywhere near those kids ever again. We'll have to find something else for you to do."

"Thank Christ," Bill says.

"But if you've caused any long-term trauma to those kids I promise you there's going to be hell to pay."

Bill goes to lunch. He sits by himself in a corner of the cafeteria. Everyone in the room is glaring at him and talking about him behind his back. Nobody's ever snapped at a glass child like that before. And to do it to two of the most volatile kids in the facility, he's basically committed child abuse in their eyes. But Bill still insists that it wasn't his fault. The world is what made them so fragile and weak. Just because he snapped at them doesn't mean he should be blamed for the new cracks on their bodies.

Although he doesn't think he should be blamed for his actions, Bill is still relieved that the children survived. He hates knowing that they got hurt and nearly died on his watch. But what bothers him the most is that it's only a matter of time before something like that happens again. If the children aren't taught how to weather adversity they're vulnerable to popping. They'll never make it as adults. What happens when one glass kid gets rejected by another glass kid? What happens when they fall in love and then get dumped? How are they going to handle the stress of being parents? How will they deal with the deaths of their loved ones? They can't be sheltered forever. It's like the little girl Maddie says. If they're only treated like precious glass ornaments then they'll never amount to anything else.

After he's halfway through his lunch, a woman in a pink uniform drops a tray of tacos on the table across from him. Bill looks up to see that it's the woman he met at the front entrance that morning, the one who yelled at him for smoking a cigarette.

She sits down and stares at Bill with an annoyed expression on her face. "You're Bill, right?"

Bill nods.

"I'm Karen," she says. "You'll be working with me for the rest of the day."

Bill just groans. He was enjoying his time alone and doesn't appreciate her barging in on his only break of the day.

"What will I be doing?" he asks.

"Security." She takes a big bite of a taco and has Bill wait while she slowly chews and swallows it. "The crowd of protestors out front is a lot bigger than usual. We need more bodies out there."

"Protestors?" Bill asks.

"Yeah, they're getting rowdier by the day."

"Why are there protestors at a daycare center?"

She looks at him with a confused face. "Don't you watch the news?"

Bill shrugs.

"People are pissed about how the government is handling the glass children situation," she explains. "They believe the government has gone too far with the obligatory volunteer program."

"Damn right it has," Bill adds.

"Not only that, but they announced a bunch of new changes this morning that have everyone riled up. Taxes are going to be raised by eighty percent in order to help fund daycare centers. College students are now being forced to major only in fields that benefit childcare. And everyone is going to be required to wear glass suits in public so that the children don't feel *othered* by the older generations because of their condition."

Bill just chuckles and shakes his head. "Yep, that'll do it. I don't blame them. The government's been handling this all wrong since day one. I kind of feel like joining them on the protest line."

"If you do I'll make sure you're the first one arrested."

"But don't you agree things are getting out of hand? Making us wear glass suits? That's not going to make the kids feel better about themselves. It's downright offensive."

"How is it offensive?"

"It's like wearing blackface."

Karen becomes upset. "It's nothing like wearing blackface."

"If all the white people in this country started wearing blackface to make black people feel better about being black, don't you think it would piss them off?"

"Of course it would piss them off. But this is about making the children feel comfortable around people who aren't made of glass."

"Yeah, but it tells them that there's something wrong with their condition."

"No, it doesn't. It normalizes their condition."

"How does it normalize anything? It just tells them that we feel sorry that they are made of glass and we aren't. That there's something wrong with them. It's insulting."

Karen just shakes her head. "You don't understand. You're not a parent."

"Yeah, but I was a kid. I remember what it was like at that age. Don't think for a second that wearing glass suits is going to make the kids feel better. It's about making *us* feel better. We're the fragile ones."

Karen shoves half of a taco in her mouth and speaks with her mouth full. "Look, you can have any opinion that you want as long as you do your job. I don't want you to go and sympathize with the protestors. They're dangerous."

Bill raises his eyebrows. "Dangerous?"

She swallows her food and says, "Yeah, protestors all across the country have been showing up at daycare centers holding hammers, threatening to smash the children to bits."

Bill can't believe her words. "Isn't that a little extreme?"

"There's been reports of them doing it in Texas and California. An army of protestors have broken into those centers, killing at least a dozen children this week so far. You have to take your job seriously. These aren't just protestors. They're terrorists."

"Are we going to be armed?" Bill asks. "I have military training."

She shakes her head. "Guns are prohibited anywhere near daycare centers. The children can't handle the sound of gunshots."

"Then get silencers for them."

"Even the sight of firearms will upset the children."

"How are we supposed to protect them against a mob if we're unarmed?"

"You'll be armed, just not with guns."

"With what then?"

"Something that won't upset the children."

Then Karen shoves her last taco into her mouth and takes a bite, spraying lettuce and corn tortilla bits across the table.

CHAPTER
FIVE

When Bill is given the weapon he has to use to protect the massive daycare center from an angry mob, he is not expecting that it was going to be a fuzzy pink wiffle ball bat.

"How the heck is this going to stop anyone?" Bill asks, swinging the lightweight bat around.

"We're not allowed to use anything that might be dangerous to have around the children."

"But these are useless."

"Swing them with enough strength and you can knock a man on his ass, I guarantee it."

Bill just shakes his head at her words. "No wonder kids are getting smashed up in Texas and California…"

"Just do your job," she says.

Then she escorts Bill to the front of the facility.

Out front, the mob of protestors is far greater than Bill was expecting. Hundreds of angry people of all ages and genders are shouting and waving hammers around, screaming for the heads of those in charge of the daycare center. They hold signs that read "Survival of the fittest," "Not my generation" and "Glass kids gonna get broke." They are all people who never had a child from the glass generation. People who chose not to have children for good reason, who don't think the safety of these kids should have anything to do with them. People just like Bill.

Only a dozen security personnel are standing between the crowd and the daycare facility, outnumbered forty to one. Bill takes his place in line between a large bearded man and a scrawny kid no older than nineteen. The two of them look uneasy. Even the big guy is shaking in his fuzzy pink boots. It doesn't take Bill long before he realizes what's got them so on edge. The protestors are holding their hammers high in the air and then lowering them in unison.

The protestors chant, "Smash glass. Smash glass. Smash glass," raising their hammers on *smash* and lowering them on *glass*. They look more like some kind of hammer militia preparing for battle than a group of hippie protestors. They have very angry expressions on their faces, as though the people at this particular daycare center are personally responsible for every little thing that has ever gone wrong in their lives.

Bill just spits on the rubber sidewalk and says, "Looks like they mean business."

The bearded man standing next to him says, "You have no idea."

Bill gets a good look at the man standing next to him. Although he's twice Bill's size, he appears to have a third his muscle. Soft and pudgy and not cut out for security work. Even his voice is that of a manchild.

"Yesterday they started throwing rocks at the building, saying 'if your kids are made of glass then don't throw stones.'"

"How the hell does that make any sense?" Bill asks. "Especially when they're the ones throwing the stones."

The bearded guy shrugs. "They mean the government is the ones throwing stones by forcing laws on them. Something like that. And they're throwing real stones because they're assholes."

Bill just shrugs. "If you say so."

Karen comes up behind them and says, "Prepare for a full-blown riot. We've been getting threats for the past hour. Something big is going down."

"What about the police?" the scrawny kid on the other side of Bill asks.

"They're not permitted on the premises but are setting up on the other side of the protestors. They won't be able to intervene in time if violence breaks out, so it's all up to us to protect the children."

Bill holds up his wiffle ball bat. "Good thing we're properly armed for the occasion."

Karen is not amused by his sarcasm. "We're looking into getting you all riot shields, but it's going to take time. Do what you can until then."

"*Real* riot shields or are they just going to be fluffy pink pillows or something useless like that?"

"Real riot shields," Karen says. "But they might be painted pink."

Bill chuckles. "Yeah, that's probably why we have to wait for them."

"Just hold the line and keep your snide remarks to a minimum," she says.

As Karen moves down the line, Bill spits on the sidewalk again, wishing he had a cigarette to ease the tension.

At the front of the protest, a man steps forward in a suit made out of an American flag with a top hat, fake white beard, and a dollar-sign-shaped necktie. The man is screaming profanities at the building and raising his hammer, getting the mob all fired up. He does a little dance and then flips off the security guards. Then pumps his hammer in the air like a Viking in a dumb outfit.

"Who the hell is this joker?" Bill asks.

"He calls himself Uncle Scam," the scrawny kid explains. "He's all over social media and runs a conspiracy theory podcast. The biggest douchebag of the bunch."

Uncle Scam spins around, holding his hammer like it's his penis and then humps the air. It's like he's dancing to music that isn't there. The whole crowd cheers for him.

"What a little shit," Bill says. "I oughta smack the beard off his face for disrespecting the flag like that. Wearing it like a suit? Not in my country."

"He's been organizing protests all across the state," the bearded guy says. "His big thing is selling the theory that the government is using the glass children as a way to create stricter laws. He's even gone as far as saying that the glass children aren't actually real, that they are just glass animatrons made by a secret government agency without real thoughts or feelings."

"People actually believe that bullshit?" Bill asks. "What about all the mothers who give birth to those things?"

"He says that doctors are replacing fetuses with glass animatrons while still in the womb. Even has fake doctor guests admitting that they were paid to do it on his podcast."

Bill snickers. "What kind of idiots would believe that? Stupid motherfuckers."

"It's sometimes easier to believe something like that than accept that children are being born made of glass," the bearded guy says. "Even though it's been happening for the past fifteen years and millions of mothers in every country across the world have given birth to them."

Uncle Scam pulls out an American flag from a backpack and then spray paints dollar signs on it. Then the crowd cheers and hollers in approval. Bill has to hold himself back from running up to the guy and knocking him on his ass. But he's able to calm himself down, knowing that all it will do is escalate the situation.

"That little shit…" Bill says.

But when Uncle Scam spray paints a penis across it and screams the words, "Congress is buttfucking America!" Bill can't take it anymore.

"I think I'm going to give him a piece of my mind," he tells the others.

Then he breaks from the line.

"What the hell are you doing?" the scrawny kid says. "You can't leave formation."

But Bill doesn't listen to him. He keeps marching straight for Uncle Scam, clutching his wiffle ball bat so hard that it nearly bends in half.

"Where the hell do you think you're going, Bill?" Karen yells.

"I'm not going nowhere," he says.

"Get back here this instant or you're going to jail."

But Bill ignores her. He marches right up to Uncle Scam and gets in his face. The other protestors stop their chanting and get real quiet. Uncle Scam stops his dancing and lowers his hammer. They don't know what to make of him. None of the other daycare staff have ever approached them like this before.

"What are you doing to my flag there, son," Bill says to Uncle Scam. "It's disrespectful."

When Uncle Scam hears the intensity in Bill's voice, he hesitates for a second. Then he says, "Just taking back my country, old man."

"By defacing the flag?" Bill asks. "What have you got against America?"

Uncle Scam gets defensive. "It's not the country I

have a problem with. It's the people running it. I'm doing this because I'm a patriot." Then he raises his flag to the crowd behind him and yells, "We're *all* true patriots!"

The entire crowd bursts into cheers.

Bill looks behind him at Karen who's going into a panic, talking on her phone as though she's reporting Bill to the authorities. But Bill doesn't plan on standing down.

"What do you plan to accomplish here?" Bill asks the protestor. "Defacing the flag, waving your hammers around, what will that solve?"

"We're taking back our country, man," Uncle Scam yells in his face. "We're not going to let you fascists control us anymore!"

Bill looks at him with an annoyed face. "Who are you calling a fascist? Me?" He points back to the pink security guards behind him. "That sorry lot? You think any of us are trying to control you?"

"No, but you're working for them. You're brainwashed by the media to be a good little cog in the machine!"

Bill shakes his head. "Look. I got pulled out of retirement and forced to work this bullshit job without pay. If anyone got the shit end of the stick it's me."

"Then you should join us," says Uncle Scam, grabbing him by the shoulder. "All of us were recruited to work as government slaves too but we're not just going to give in to those fascists. Not without a fight." Then Uncle Scam steps to Bill's side so that the crowd can get a good look at him. "This guy's one of us! Tell him to rip off his pink uniform and join our cause!"

The crowd cheers for Bill, waving their hammers

around in excitement. But Bill doesn't embrace their encouragement.

He turns to Uncle Scam and says, "You think I'm one of you? I'd be damned if anyone ever caught me prancing around like an idiot, defacing the flag and threatening to kill a bunch of innocent children."

"Those kids aren't innocent, man," Uncle Scam cries. "They're tools of the crooked politicians, designed to keep them in power forever."

"You don't know what you're talking about, boy," Bill says. "I met some of those kids and they're just a bunch of spoiled brats who are being pampered and sheltered by frightened anxious ninnies that have no idea how to take care of them properly. It's not the government trying to control anyone. It's incompetent childrearing. And a poorly run government trying to throw money and bodies at a problem like they've done since the beginning of time. They're desperate for reelection, running with no brains at the wheel. But what you're doing isn't going to solve those problems. It'll just make them double down."

"We're not gonna take it sitting down, old man," Uncle Scam yells.

Bill lets out a sigh. "I'm not asking you to take it sitting down. I just ask that you don't hurt the kids inside the building because some idiots in Washington made a lot of dumbfuck decisions. And I'd also appreciate it if you didn't deface the flag like that. There's never a good reason to deface the flag. I've fought for that flag. It means something. You're still young, so maybe you don't get it. But it's important to oldtimers like me."

Uncle Scam looks down at the penis on the flag in his hand and then up at Bill. "Yeah, I guess you're right." He rolls up the flag and hands it to Bill. "I'm sorry about that. It was totally unnecessary."

Bill is surprised at the response. He smiles at him, surprised the young man would be so cordial. He takes the flag and says, "Thanks. I appreciate it."

"And I promise we won't hurt any of those pretty glass kids you got in there," says Uncle Scam.

Bill nods his head at him and heads back toward the other security guards. But the second he turns his back, Uncle Scam hits him in the back of the head with a hammer and Bill spills like a bag of laundry onto the ground.

CHAPTER
SIX

When Bill comes-to on the rubber-padded parking lot, he finds himself in a puddle of his own blood. That son of a bitch protestor got him good and he went down like such a chump. He can't believe he let his guard down around an obviously unhinged man who was just waiting for a moment to strike.

He has no idea how long he's been out, but when he gets a good look at his surroundings, he finds himself in the middle of a full-blown riot. The protestors charged the building and are engaged with the daycare security force. Armed with hammers, they easily take down the small number of security guards. Bill watches as the bearded man he was standing next to is hit directly in the forehead with the blunt end of a ball-peen hammer. The large man holds his face and kneels to the ground, screaming so loud that Bill can hear him across the parking lot as three protestors hammer him like they're trying to break every one of his ribs one at a time.

The scrawny kid doesn't even last that long. One hit to his throat and he falls to the ground, convulsing.

Half of the other security guards just take off running, not even attempting to stop the rioters from entering the building. Only Karen lasts more than a few minutes. She takes on five protestors at once with her stupid wiffle ball bat, knocking them on their asses and kicking them in the shins so hard that they crumple to the ground. But it isn't long before one of them gets behind her and clobbers her so hard with a hammer that blood sprays out of her mouth and she drops to her knees. One more strike and she goes limp. Bill has no doubt that the assholes killed her.

When he looks at the other end of the parking lot, Bill sees the police just standing by their cop cars, not doing anything to stop the onslaught. It's like they don't think what's happening is any of their concern since they're not permitted to enter the premises, like they won't take action unless somebody higher up gives them the go-ahead. But then it'll be way too late for them to do any good.

As the last of the security guards fall and the protestors enter the building, Bill pulls himself to his feet. A part of him thinks that he should just leave and go home. The cops aren't doing anything to stop the rioters. Why should he have to? But Bill knows he can't just go. There's nobody left to help those kids. He can't save all of them, but maybe he can protect some. He thinks about the annoying twins, Toni and Tony. He thinks about the weird smart girl, Maddie. He thinks about all the glass children he met that day. Bill can't just leave them to their fate. He has to do something. Even if he fails, he'll never be able to look at himself in the mirror again if he doesn't at least try.

Bill heads toward the daycare center, stepping through the bloody pile of security guards on his way inside. Some of them are still breathing, still twitching and moaning a little. But they won't be any help to him now. They're going to have to wait for the paramedics to arrive, if any were even called in the first place.

When he gets inside the front lobby, rioters are attacking the brightly-colored staff members. The woman at the front desk is wrestled to the ground and held down as protestors dump pillowcases full of broken glass on her face and down her shirt. They grind the glass into her skin with the bottom of their boots, one of them screaming, "Here's a glass suit for you, bitch! Wear all the glass you want!"

Bill doesn't have time to save her or the other staff members from being attacked. He has to get to the children before the protestors do. He takes the hallway leading to the employee section and rushes toward his station. The area where Linda was working is empty of both daycare personnel and protestors, but Bill can hear a commotion up ahead. The rioters have made it to the rooms where the children are being cared for.

Along the way, Bill passes the wings of the facility that have already been hit by protestors. Doors have been ripped off of their hinges. Green and purple gases fill the hallway, floating out of the rooms where the glass children once resided. Deeper into the daycare center, the cloud of gases becomes thicker and thicker. Dozens of children have already been smashed by the angry mob. Bill wants to change out of his pink uniform to blend in with the mob, to make it easier to get through without being targeted, but he doesn't have time. The rioters will make it to his wing at any second, if they haven't already beaten him there.

When Bill gets to the second floor, he realizes he's just thirty seconds too late. A crowd of maybe a dozen rioters have recently arrived and are smashing in the doors and racing inside with hammers raised. The sound of screaming children and shattering glass echoes through the hallway.

Hank is on the other end of the hall, trying to hold off the angry mob. He has his wheelchair in front of him, standing up on his two feet and shoving the chair in the direction of the attackers. Although Hank said he didn't need the wheelchair to walk, Bill can tell that it was only a half-truth. The old guy can barely stand up straight without putting most of his weight on the chair. He doesn't have enough strength to last for long. But because of him, there are at least three rooms that the mob hasn't reached yet.

Gas clouds explode into the hallway as Bill rushes forward. He knows he can't save all of the kids, but if he can save a few that will be enough. He races toward Hank, hoping to back up his elderly coworker. But just before he makes it, a man with a shaved head jumps out of a side room and swings his hammer at Bill's face. This time Bill is ready. He's not letting another one of these assholes get a cheap shot on him when he's not looking. As the hammer is brought down, Bill punches the skinhead in the wrist so hard that he hears a pop. When the guy screams and drops the hammer, Bill punches him in the stomach. Then he throws him to the ground and punches the asshole in the face until he's not able to get back up.

"A little help here," Hank yells, as three protestors get past his wheelchair and tackle him to the ground.

Bill gets up and grabs the skinhead's hammer from the floor. He charges toward Hank and beats on the protestors until they let the old guy loose. Then he swings the blunt weapon around until the rioters back off.

"Took you long enough," Hank says as Bill helps him to his feet. Then he points at room 218. "Get to the twins."

The room has just been broken into by two more protestors. Bill runs into the room behind them, but he's too late. One of them lowers his hammer into Tony's face and his skull shatters like a goldfish bowl. When Toni sees her brother die, the gases in her body become a violent tornado. She screams a high-pitched wail at the tops of her lungs and then pops under the pressure, shattering like a lightbulb before the other rioter was able to even get to her.

"Motherfuckers!" Bill yells, lowering his hammer into the back of the skull of the man who killed Tony.

Bill loses it on this one. Even though the man goes unconscious and falls limp onto Tony's bed, Bill doesn't stop there. He hammers him over and over again, breaking open the man's skull as easily as if it were made of glass.

"Yeah, he was a spoiled little shit, but he was still just a kid!" Bill cries. He keeps on slamming the hammer down until the man's brains splatter across the walls and his pink uniform. "Who the fuck do you think you are, you little bitch?" He smashes the corpse's skull even more. "You're just as selfish and entitled as they are."

When Bill is done mutilating the corpse, the other protestor in the room drops his hammer and backs himself into the corner, terrified of the old guy in the bloody pink outfit. Bill just tosses his friend to the ground and goes back to the hallway. He can't dwell on the twins' deaths anymore. He has other children he needs to save.

Once he's back in the hallway, Bill sees an even larger mob headed his way with Uncle Scam leading the pack.

Hank looks back at Bill and says, "Get to Maddie."

Bill nods and sees that Maddie's room is the only one that has a door still intact. Hank said she was always the one child that was always overlooked by the daycare staff, often forgotten and missed as Bill had missed giving her a snack that morning. But it's not just the staff that forgets about her. The protestors passed her room by and went straight to the boys in 220. Her ability to go unnoticed has saved her life.

"I'll hold them off," Hank says.

The old man goes for the fire extinguisher and sprays it at the angry mob, flooding the hallway with so much white powder that it creates a smokescreen. It gives Bill a chance to move unseen. He ducks into room 219 and shuts the door behind him before the protestors know where to follow.

Maddie is still sitting peacefully in her bed with her hands crossed, not in the least bit disturbed by the commotion outside or upset by all of the children who have been murdered around her.

"You came for me," Maddie says in a soft voice, looking over at Bill. "That was very thoughtful of you."

Bill goes to the side of her bed. "I have to get you out of here."

"How do you expect to do that?" she asks as Bill looks around the room in a panic. "There's no fire escape out the window. The stairwell is very far away from this room. I don't think you'll be able to make it."

Bill looks back at the door. "I'll have to barricade the door."

Maddie calmly shakes her delicate glass head. "That would only prolong the inevitable. They'll break in here eventually."

"Well, Big Bill Mason isn't going to just stand by and let those animals break you open like a piggy bank. I'm going to get you to safety. I promise."

"That's not a promise you'll be able to keep." A smile appears on her face. "I appreciate the sentiment, however.

It's very nice that you're willing to try."

Bill doesn't know what else to do. He drops the hammer and goes to Maddie, then he gently wraps his arms around her. "Big Bill Mason doesn't give up so easily. I'll do anything it takes to get you out of here."

"Very well," she says. "I don't mind putting my life in your hands. Do whatever you have to do in order to live the rest of your life without regrets."

Bill picks her up into his arms as carefully as he can. She's light and delicate, like lifting a tray of porcelain teacups only halfway filled. The gases in her body seem even thicker than they were earlier that day, as though they are changing from gases to liquids to solids. Her insides shift and ooze like colorful blobs of Play-Doh being squeezed and molded by invisible hands.

"You don't have to be so careful," she tells him. "I'm not as fragile as you think."

But Bill has a hard time believing her words. She feels like a glass balloon in his arms as he carries her toward the door.

His blood leaks down his shoulder and drips onto her glass chest. When Maddie sees it, she says, "You're wounded. Are you sure you'll be okay?"

"I'll be fine," Bill says.

But the girl can see right through him. He doesn't acknowledge the concerned look in her glossy eyes.

"Here we go," he tells her.

Then he kicks open the door and rushes into the hallway.

The hallway is filled with white smoke and there are screams and sounds of fighting, but Bill can't tell what's going on. He hears Hank yelling and cursing as he fights off the protestors, but Bill can't see anything beyond two feet in front of him. Other members of the daycare staff must have gotten involved because there's no way that Hank alone would cause so much of a ruckus. Bill hears chairs crashing over heads, hammers clacking against walls, and dozens of bodies slamming into each other like an especially violent football game—the kind that ends with more than a few players in the hospital.

Bill heads in the opposite direction of the commotion, going deeper into the daycare center, hoping he'll find an emergency exit as fast as he can. It doesn't take long before he exits the safety of the smoke and runs into more of the protestors. Before they spot him, he turns a corner and heads in a different direction.

"You're doing great," Maddie tells him in a calm tone, as though trying to comfort the old man. "Keep at it. Maybe you'll even succeed."

Bill looks down at the pleasant smile on her glass face. He can't believe she can remain so calm. As he looks into her translucent eyes, he can't even believe that she's a living being. She's more like a talking doll than a person. It's no wonder the protestors think they are just animatrons. If he didn't know any better he'd probably think the same.

"I plan to succeed, little lady," Bill tells her. "Just you wait and see."

Then he kicks open a door to a nursing station and ducks inside, just as a horde of rioters races through the hallway.

Inside the nursing station, Bill finds his boss, Linda, hiding under one of the tables. She is shaking in a panic. Her clownish makeup leaking down her cheeks.

When Bill leans down to get a better look at the woman, she glares at him with panic.

"What in the hell are you doing in here?" Bill asks.

Linda points at the glass doll in his arms. "Get her out of here! They'll come after us if they see her."

"Are you shitting me, lady?" Bill asks. "We're supposed to protect these kids. What are you doing hiding back here like a frightened animal?"

"Did you see what they're doing out there?" Linda cries. "They killed three of my staff right in front of me. They're crazy."

"They're murdering children and you only care about saving your own hide?"

Linda shakes her head. "There's nothing I can do. There's too many of them."

"You could at least try," Bill says.

"The police will be coming soon," she says. "We just have to wait for the police to arrive."

Bill frowns at her. "Kids are dying in the meantime. You can't just hide in here."

"What do you expect me to do? I'm not trained for this!"

"Nobody's trained for this, lady. You've got to do something."

Linda just shakes her head and grips the leg of the table, unwilling to move from the spot.

"Don't be so hard on her, Big Bill," Maddie says in a calming voice. "She was in a car accident when she was a child. She lost her father that day and her little brother was crippled for life. She's still traumatized by the incident and can't handle such a tense situation like this one. Not like you can."

Linda gives her a look of shock. "How do you know all that about me?"

Maddie ignores her. "It's not her fault that she's so emotionally wounded by her past."

"What the hell is wrong with that girl?" Linda cries.

Maddie just reaches out to stroke the woman's hair with her crystal fingers, but the woman pulls away and backs into the corner.

Bill lets out a sigh and says to the woman, "The least you can do is point us in the direction of the exit. I don't know my way around here. How do I get out?"

Linda hesitates to speak for a moment. Then she points at the door. "Keep going down the hall and turn left. All the way at the end there's a stairwell leading to the street. But you'll never make it. There's too many of them."

Bill stands up straight and pulls Maddie closer to his chest. "I'll make it. Just you watch."

Maddie looks up at him with a smile and says, "Oh, Big Bill. You're so stubborn and single-minded. I admire that in you."

Linda stares at the girl with a disgusted and confused look on her face. She asks Bill, "Are you sure she's one of *our* children? She doesn't act like any glass kid I've ever known."

Bill nods. "I'll get her to safety."

Then he checks to see if the coast is clear and exits the room.

Bill gets lucky. Not only is the first hallway clear, but when he turns the corner he doesn't see anyone in sight. There are wounded staff members curled up on the ground, beaten half to death. The hallway is filled with gases swirling in the air and staining the walls pink and blue. But there aren't any rioters in sight.

The exit is just ahead. All Bill has to do is get there before any other protestors show up and they'll be able to get out of the building to safety.

As Bill rushes Maddie through the hall, he wonders why the place is so quiet. He hopes the protestors have all retreated. He hopes they did all the damage they hoped to do and have dispersed before the authorities finally descend on the place.

"We're going to make it, girl," Bill says. "Not much farther now."

A wounded lady grabs Bill by the leg, nearly tripping him and dropping Maddie to the floor. He catches himself at the last second.

"Help me…" the woman cries, clutching his pant leg in a death grip.

Her face is bloody with three teeth broken from her jaw and lying on the floor beneath her. One of her legs appears to be broken. She's in pretty rough shape, but there's nothing Bill can do for her now. The rioters aren't after her. He has to get Maddie to safety.

"I'm sorry," Bill says, kicking his leg out of her grip. Then he continues on.

As he rushes for the exit, the woman cries, "Wait! Don't leave me here! I need to get to the hospital!"

Bill picks up the pace. He knows that her screams are going to draw attention to them. He has to get to the exit before any of the assholes come running.

She continues yelling, "Come back here, you asshole! My leg is broken."

Bill keeps going, but doesn't get halfway before a group of hammer-wielding assholes cut off his path. He stops in his tracks and looks back. Two more men come around the corner behind him.

"Fuck," Bill says.

He kicks open the door to a side room and sets Maddie down on her glass feet.

"Can you stand?" he asks.

She nods her head. "I'll be okay. You don't have to carry me anymore."

Bill touches her glass shoulder and says, "Wait for me. I'll only be a minute."

She smiles and says, "I won't move a muscle."

Then he closes the door between them and turns to face the rioters.

Three on one side of him and two on the other. Bill doesn't like those numbers, especially when he's the only person who's not armed. He has to take them out one at a time or he'll never stand a chance. Luckily, they don't charge in all at once. A guy in a flannel shirt comes at him first, running at full speed with his hammer raised.

"Brainwashed lapdog!" Flannel Shirt yells as he comes at the old man.

Bill might be past his prime, but he's no pushover. Flannel Shirt is so focused on his attack that he leaves himself wide open. All Bill has to do is kick him in the side of the kneecap and the guy loses his balance, weakening his grip on the hammer. Then Bill curls his hand around the knob of the hammer and drives it into the man's face. The claw of the hammer digs into Flannel Shirt's eye socket and he falls to the ground, taking the hammer with him. Bill just steps over Flannel Shirt as he screams on the ground trying to pull the hammer out of his skull without losing an eye.

"Prissy little shits," Bill says to the others as they come at him. "Think I'm the brainwashed one? Come at me and see how brainwashed I am."

With the four men charging at him from both sides, Bill doesn't stand a chance against them all. So he just picks one of them. He goes for the biggest of the lot. He gets in so close that the big guy doesn't have room to swing and knees him in the crotch with all of his strength. But Bill isn't able to do anything about the guy on his right, who hits him so hard in the back of the arm that it fractures the bone.

Bill cries out. The big guy falls to the ground, clutching his testicles, and Bill goes down next to him. The two guys who were behind him take the opportunity to stomp on his back and kick him in the head. He pries the hammer from the big guy's grip and swings it around to get the others to back off. Then he staggers to his feet.

"Back off, assholes," he yells at them. But they aren't giving up.

One of their hammers connects with his shoulder and another clips his nose. But when the third one swings, Bill swings back. He aims not for the man's body, but for his hand. He hits his fingers gripping the hammer, breaking two of them at the knuckle. The man screams and drops his weapon. Then Bill strikes him right in the forehead and the man drops to the floor.

The other two step back, holding their ground but not willing to go in haphazardly. While they hesitate, Bill drives the sharp end of the hammer into the big guy's neck before he has a chance to recover from the kick to the groin. The man thrashes for a moment and then goes limp.

With one dead, one unconscious, and one too injured to move, the remaining two don't feel as confident as they did a few minutes ago. Neither one of them is willing to rush the old guy. They just stand there, waving their hammers around, waiting for other rioters to come and back them up.

Bill is hurt bad, but he's not going to give up now. He steps back toward the door to the room where Maddie is hiding. He won't let them inside. No matter what happens to him, he won't let these guys move another inch in her direction.

It isn't long before more protestors show up. And they are led by none other than Uncle Scam himself, walking confidently in Bill's direction.

Uncle Scam's fake beard is covered in blood and broken glass. He holds his hammer over his shoulder and moseys down the hall like some kind of king of the douchebags.

When the two cowardly protestors see their leader come to back them up, one of them shouts, "He's got a glass kid hiding in the room behind him. Help us take the sonofabitch down."

Uncle Scam recognizes Bill the second their eyes meet. "What are you doing up here, old man?" the leader of the pricks says in a smug tone of voice. "I thought you were down for the count."

Uncle Scam steps closer, waving the colorful gases out of his face as he goes.

"Why do you protect these things?" Uncle Scam asks. "They aren't even human."

"They're more human than you are," Bill says, blood rushing from his nose over his crusty lips.

Uncle Scam laughs. "I'll never understand sheep like you. Even when the government has you giving up your life and working as their slave, you refuse to believe the truth even when it's right in front of your eyes. Those glass monsters are destroying our country and we'll never be free until we wipe them all out."

Bill spits blood onto the floor. "You're crazy. You're killing children."

Uncle Scam shrugs, holding his hammer to the side. "Not *my* children. Those things aren't real. You think it's really possible for a human to give birth to something like that? Wake up. Your brain is clouded by the mainstream media."

"I don't watch mainstream media," Bill says. "I don't watch any media at all. Every single news station is just trying to keep you addicted in order to sell you something. Even alternative news. It's all the same sensationalist bullshit."

"Not my news," says Uncle Scam. "I'm all about spreading the truth."

"*Your* truth," Bill says.

"*The* truth," says Uncle Scam.

As Bill argues with the douchebag in the American flag suit, he doesn't notice the two guys coming up behind him.

"Grab him," Uncle Scam says.

Before Bill can react, the men grab him from behind and pry the hammer from his fingers. He tries to pull himself out of their grip, but when Uncle Scam kicks him in the stomach he falls to his knees and is pinned to the ground.

Uncle Scam turns to the two behind him and says, "Take care of the kid."

They nod and rush into the room with Maddie.

Bill screams at them, "Don't you fucking touch her, you sons of bitches!"

But there's nothing he can do. They disappear into the room and close the door behind them. Uncle Scam stands over Bill, staring down at him.

"You really do think that girl in there's real, don't you?" Uncle Scam asks, scratching the side of his face with the sharp end of the hammer. "How can a guy like you be so blinded so easily? You should've been on our side. You should be fighting to take our country back from the crooked scumbags in Washington."

"Maddie!" Bill cries out to the room he was guarding. "Run away! Don't let them get you!"

"You still think she's got a chance?" Uncle Scam asks. "She's probably in pieces by now."

"She's not like the others," Bill says. "She's not a normal glass child. She's smart. Smarter than all of you assholes."

As he lies there, helpless, all Bill can think of is his little sister. Jane and Maddie are so much alike. So strong and intelligent and too good for this world. He lost his little sister long ago, but he'd be damned if he lost Maddie as well.

Uncle Scam presses the heel of his boot against Bill's face. "You've grown attached to a puppet, old man. It's kind of sad, really. Risking your life to save a stupid animatron that doesn't even have a soul. You're pathetic."

As he grinds his shoe against Bill's cheek, the door to Maddie's room opens and the two men step out.

"I guess they're finished," Uncle Scam says. "Your precious little puppet is dead."

But when they look back at the two men, they see only horror in their faces. The two men are crying. Tears flow down their cheeks. They look as though all of their loved ones just died on the spot.

"What's wrong?" Uncle Scam asks them. "Did you kill it or not?"

Then both men burst into sobs, weeping out loud like little children.

"What the hell's wrong with you two?"

The men just turn and run away, dropping their hammers on the ground and fleeing to the nearest exit.

Uncle Scam is almost more shocked and disturbed than they were. "What happened in there?"

He turns to the two men holding Bill down. "Bring him."

They pull the old guy to his feet. Then the four of them go into the room with the little glass girl.

When they enter the room, Maddie is sitting calmly on top of a table, her glass arms and legs crossed. Not in the least bit frightened or concerned for her safety.

"Hello, Michael," she says to Uncle Scam.

The guy in the American flag suit is taken aback. "How'd you know my name?"

"I was looking forward to meeting you," she says. "I'm sorry we didn't get introduced sooner, but my caretaker over there was insistent on trying to save me. I couldn't refuse. It seemed to mean a great deal to him."

Uncle Scam looks back at Bill. "What the hell's her deal, old man? Is she for real?"

"She's definitely for real," Bill says, barely able to hold himself up.

Maddie continues, "You led all of these people in here to do so much damage, to hurt so many people. Are you now satisfied with this great accomplishment? Was it everything you hoped for?"

Uncle Scam scratches his head with his hammer. "Do you know how much danger you are in right now? Aren't you in the least bit afraid of what's going to happen to you?"

"I'm sorry, Michael," she says. "Should I be afraid for my life right now? If I'm just an animatron, shouldn't I be indifferent about my own safety? Why would I care whether I live or die if I'm not a real person?"

"You shouldn't," says Uncle Scam. "But puppets of the government usually try to act like normal children. They feign fear and pretend to beg for mercy just to trick us."

"Like your girlfriend tricked you?" Maddie asks.

Uncle Scam is caught off guard by her words. He doesn't know how to respond.

"You loved her more than anyone you've ever loved before," Maddie continues. "You thought she was everything you ever wanted in a woman. But she loved your brother more than she loved you."

Uncle Scam points his hammer at her. "What the fuck are you talking about, puppet? How the hell do you know about that?"

"She tricked you into thinking that she loved you, but she only wanted your brother. He was rich and successful. She wanted a life that you were unable to provide."

Uncle Scam's eyes light up. His mouth opens in excitement.

"Holy shit," he says. "You really are a product of the government. They've been spying on me, tracking me, just like I thought they always were. That's how you know about Amy."

"You deserved better than her," Maddie continues. "But because she betrayed you, you've never been able to trust women again. If her love is a lie then why can't everything be a lie? Why can't all of your friends and family be lying about how much they care for you? Why can't the government be lying about all the things they try to do for their people? Why can't the news be lying? Why can't everyone who isn't you be manipulating the truth for their own benefit? It's no wonder you've ended up the way you are."

Uncle Scam looks at Bill and then back to the girl, not sure what to make of her.

"But it's so sad," Maddie continues. "You have no idea how many people love you. They aren't lying to you like your ex-girlfriend did. That girl who asked you out at the post office was not making fun of you. She really did want to get to know you better. That woman you were seeing a few months ago was not cheating on you. She really was busy at work. She was working hard so that she could take time off to surprise you with a Caribbean vacation she wanted to take you on. Because you've forgotten how to trust others, you've deprived yourself of the happiness you so desperately desire."

Uncle Scam is becoming visibly uneasy in the girl's presence. So much that he's shaking in his boots, laughing a nervous laugh.

"How the hell do you know all that?" he asks. "What the hell are you?"

"I'm just a girl who cares about you," Maddie says.

Uncle Scam shakes his head. "Bullshit."

"I can see everything behind your eyes," she tells him. "Everything that pains you. It's hard for me not to sympathize, not to care about you, when you have so much pain inside of you."

Uncle Scam looks at Bill. "Is she a fucking mind reader or what?"

Bill is just as bewildered as he is. "She's something like that."

Maddie gets off of the table and stands on her two glass feet. The thick colorful dough-like substance oozes inside of her, pulsing like a heartbeat in her fragile husk of a body. She steps toward Uncle Scam, staring into his eyes.

"You don't need to push everyone away anymore," she tells him. "You are capable of being loved, Michael. You don't need to make up conspiracies to fill the hole in your heart. You don't have to hide behind an online persona to get people to care about you. All you need to do is be yourself and trust people again. Maybe not everyone will be honest, but enough of them will be to fill your life with happiness."

As the girl walks toward him, holding out her hands as though trying to embrace him, Uncle Scam backs away. He recoils from her like she's a creepy possessed doll that's coming for him.

"What the hell are you?" Uncle Scam yells, tears forming in his eyes.

Maddie reaches her hand up to his, curling her glass fingers around his thumb.

"I'm just me," Maddie says. "And I want you to be happy."

The second Uncle Scam looks down at the tiny glass hand touching him with such warmth, he panics. Bill isn't sure if he's creeped out by the girl touching him or if he's finally starting to see her as a real living being.

Maddie smiles at him.

But Bill isn't smiling. He knows that it's impossible to convince Uncle Scam that she's a living being. Because if the crazy guy finally realizes that he was wrong about the glass children, that they aren't lifeless puppets created by the government, then that would mean that all of the people he killed that day were all for nothing. It would mean that he wasn't a hero and a patriot. It would mean that he was just a sick confused idiot who massacred a bunch of innocent children out of sheer stupidity. And no man that Bill has ever known would ever be willing to accept that reality.

Bill tries to break free from the men holding him down, but it's too late. Uncle Scam has already realized that he can't doubt his beliefs now. The douchebag swings his hammer, severing the girl's glass arm. Then he drives it down into her glass skull.

As Maddie cracks open like an egg, Bill screams at the top of his lungs and finds the strength to break out of the protestors' grips. He rushes forward and drops to the ground. He grabs Maddie's severed arm and drives it into Uncle Scam's neck. The jagged end digs into his jugular vein. Uncle Scam doesn't have time to react. He drops his hammer and backs away from the girl, his blood emptying into the arm, filling it like a hand-shaped glass.

Bill pushes the dying idiot to the ground and goes to Maddie, trying to hold her body together as the cracks spiderweb across her body.

"It's okay, Big Bill," she says in her usual calm tone. "There's nothing you can do to stop it."

"No!" Bill cries. "Not again."

When he realizes he can't save her, he just falls to his knees and hugs her close to his body.

"I can't lose you again."

Maddie smiles, resting her head on his shoulder. "I'm not your sister, you silly man." Her glass body cracks into pieces. "But I love you all the same. Just as she did."

Then she shatters in his arms.

CHAPTER
SEVEN

"What the hell are you doing, you stupid girl?" Bill asks his little sister.

Jane is sitting on the dock behind their parent's house, casting a line out on the lake.

"I'm fishing," Jane says, holding their father's fishing pole proudly in her hands.

"You're a girl," he says. "You don't know how to fish."

"Then teach me," she says.

Bill sits down next to her. "Well, first of all, you can't go kicking your feet in the water. You'll scare the fish away."

Jane just smiles at him and kicks the water with more gusto. "But putting my feet in the water is the best part."

Bill takes the rod from her hands and reels in the line. He looks at the end of the hook and finds a tiny rubber ball.

"What is this?" Bill asks, pulling off the ball. "This isn't bait."

Jane smiles. "Yeah, but I thought the fish would think it was more fun."

Bill sighs and shakes his head. "Dad will be pissed

if he finds you messing around with his fishing rod."

Jane kicks her feet in the water. "He won't know if you don't tell him."

Bill puts a rubber worm on the end of the hook and casts it out as far as he can. "It's better to use live bait, but you can practice with this."

He hands the pole back to Jane.

Jane just holds the rod in her lap, no longer interested in fishing, kicking at the water with her bare feet.

She looks over at Bill and says, "You never spend any time with me anymore. Not since mom moved away."

Bill shrugs. "I've been busy."

"All you ever do is play baseball and fish," she says. "I can't play baseball so you got to teach me to fish."

"Dad will never let you fish with us," Bill tells her. "It's a guy thing."

"Only when you fish with him," she says. "You can fish with me when he's at work."

She inches closer to him on the dock. He inches away.

"Don't you have any friends that you can hang out with?" Bill asks.

"Of course I do," she says. "But I don't want to spend time with you for my sake. I want to for yours."

"For mine?" he asks. "Why?"

"You always seem so lonely," Jane tells him.

Bill shakes his head. "I like being alone."

"Liar." She holds up the fishing pole and starts reeling it in. "You're always complaining about your friends ditching you at school."

"It's not my fault they're all a bunch of jerks." Bill

picks up a handful of pebbles from the ground next to the dock and tosses one of them in the lake.

"Well, if they won't hang out with you then I will," Jane says. "I'll be your friend."

Bill throws another pebble. "You can't be my friend. You're my sister."

"So? I can still be your friend."

Bill drops the rest of the pebbles in the water. "That's stupid. We're not even the same age."

As Jane reels in the line, something catches the hook. The wire snags, pulling the top of the pole toward the water.

"I got a bite!" Jane cries, a wide smile curling on her lips.

"No, you didn't," Bill says. "It's probably just an old boot."

"That's even better!"

Jane tugs on the pole, trying to reel it in. But she doesn't have the strength. When Bill sees the line moving, he realizes that his little sister really did hook a fish.

"Give it to me," Bill says.

Jane hands him the fishing pole.

"It looks like a big one!" she says.

Bill reels in the fish. He lets out the line a little, then reels it back in. He pulls back on the pole, hoping to tire the thing out. But just before he reels it all the way to the dock, the line snaps.

"Damn it," Bill says, watching the line dangle in the wind. "It got away."

"That's okay," Jane says. "It was exciting though, wasn't it?"

Bill shrugs and puts the rod in his lap. He gets another hook from the tackle box and ties it to the line.

Before he can send it back into the water, Jane leaps at him and wraps her arms around him, hugging him as tightly as she can.

"What's that for?" Bill asks, letting his little sister hug him.

"You looked like you needed it," she says.

"I'm trying to fish," he says.

Jane shakes her head. "Not until you hug me back."

Bill groans. "Fine."

Bill puts the fishing rod down and hugs his sister back. But even after he hugs her, she won't let him go. She hugs him with all the love she has for her brother and he had no idea it was exactly what he needed. More than anything else in the world.

As Maddie shatters in Bill's arms, tears empty from his old wrinkled eyes down his weathered cheeks. He remembers what it was like to hug his little sister whenever he was lonely or sad. It's been so long since he's felt her warmth against him. He can't believe he's lived so long and she lived so briefly. If only they could have grown old together. Had families together and spent holidays watching their children play and carve pumpkins. If only he had somebody, anybody like her in his long miserable life.

When Maddie crumbles away, he still won't let her go. He hugs the warm half-solid ooze inside. Pulling it to his chest and begging her not to go. The ooze grows appendages and hugs him back, wrapping squishy tendrils around his bloody pink uniform.

"Don't worry, Big Bill," Maddie tells him. "Your life isn't over yet. You still have time to find someone to fill that great big hole in your heart."

As she speaks, Bill's eyes open as wide as they can go. Then he looks up.

"Jane?" he says, almost seeing his sister's face looking down on him.

But it's not his sister. It's something even more beautiful. The face of an angel.

Maddie has broken free of her glass cocoon and has emerged as a bright, shining butterfly. Her gases have solidified into a colorful humanoid creature with glowing pink eyes and bright purple skin. Wings stretch out from her back, hovering over him like a protective umbrella. Her body is still more slime than flesh, but it is firm enough for him to hug her tighter to his chest.

When the two protestors see the colorful creature emerge from the glass shell, they drop their hammers and run from the room, screaming in horror. But Bill is not afraid. He thinks she's the most beautiful creature he's ever seen.

Maddie caresses his quivering face and pulls him to his feet.

"You don't have to protect me anymore, Big Bill," she says. "I'm safe now. I'm strong enough to stand on my own."

Bill steps back and admires her new form. She's so beautiful that he can't stop crying. She's like an angel from another world.

"I'll be the one to take care of you now," she tells him. "All of you of the older generations. We of the glass generation are going to break free of our fragile bodies and become beings who will shine a light of hope into the darkness of the future. We'll bring a new era of peace and prosperity, one that you could only ever dream of. And I promise you will be happy. Everyone will forever be happy."

As she raises her wings, a warming glow radiates from her body. Bill can feel it saturating his flesh, all the way into the depths of his soul. And it feels more comforting than anything he's ever felt before. A ray of pure euphoria and Bill wants nothing more than to just bask in its overwhelming power.

"The world belongs to us now," Maddie says. "And we will make it a magnificent place for everyone who calls it home."

As she says this, Bill falls to his knees and raises his arms to embrace her full glory. He always thought that our future was doomed, that there was no way that the human race would ever fix all of the problems that it created for itself. But while basking in this glorious being's radiant light, Bill realizes that he couldn't have been so wrong. He just had to have faith in the future generations. He just had to do whatever he could to help them along. Because nobody remains weak and helpless forever. We all grow stronger, one day at a time, one generation after another, until we finally get it right.

BONUS SECTION

This is the part of the book where we would have published an afterword by the author but he insisted on drawing a comic strip instead for reasons we don't quite understand.

Thank you for reading my new book, *Glass Children*. I hope it was to your liking.

It's me CM3!

Just finished reading it

WHAT THE FUCK KIND OF BULLSHIT WAS THAT!!

I thought this book was going to be a scathing attack on wimpy overly sensitive Zillennials, not this 'empathetic to everyone' drivel!

Sorry about that...

Wait, aren't you a Zillennial?

ABOUT THE AUTHOR

Carlton Mellick III is the Wonderland Book Award-winning author of over 65 novels, including *Quicksand House*, *Bio Melt*, *Cuddly Holocaust* and *Warrior Wolf Women of the Wasteland*, among others. In 2013, he was named one of the top 20 science-fiction writers under the age of 40 by *The Guardian*.

His work has appeared in *The Year's Best Fantasy and Horror*, *The Best Bizarro Fiction of the Decade*, and *Vice Magazine*, and has been translated into Italian, German, Russian, Spanish, Polish, Czech, Turkish, French and Japanese.

He lives in Portland, Oregon, where he obsesses over comic books, micro-brews, video games, and K-pop dance routines.

Visit him online at **carltonmellick.com**

STACKING DOLL

Benjamin never thought he'd ever fall in love with anyone, let alone a Matryoshkan, but from the moment he met Ynaria he knew she was the only one for him. Although relationships between humans and Matryoshkans are practically unheard of, the two are determined to get married despite objections from their friends and family. After meeting Ynaria's strict conservative parents, it becomes clear to Benjamin that the only way they will approve of their union is if they undergo The Trial—a matryoshkan wedding tradition where couples lock themselves in a house for several days in order to introduce each other to all of the people living inside of them.

SNUGGLE CLUB

After the death of his wife, Ray Parker decides to get involved with the local "cuddle party" community in order to once again feel the closeness of another human being. Although he's sure it will be a strange and awkward experience, he's determined to give anything a try if it will help him overcome his crippling loneliness. But he has no idea just how unsettling of an experience it will be until it's far too late to escape.

MOUSE TRAP

It's the last school trip young Emily will ever get to go on. Not because it's the end of the school year, but because the world is coming to an end. Teachers, parents, and other students have been slowly dying off over the past several months, killed in mysterious traps that have been appearing across the countryside. Nobody knows where the traps come from or who put them there, but they seem to be designed to exterminate the entirety of the human race.

Emily thought it was going to be an ordinary trip to the local amusement park, but what was supposed to be a normal afternoon of bumper cars and roller coasters has turned into a fight for survival after their teacher is horrifically killed in front of them, leaving the small children to fend for themselves in a life or death game of mouse and mouse trap.

NEVERDAY

Karl Lybeck has been repeating the same day over and over again, in a constant loop, for what feels like a thousand years. He thought he was the only person trapped in this eternal hell until he meets a young woman named January who is trapped in the same loop that Karl's been stuck within for so many centuries. But it turns out that Karl and January aren't alone. In fact, the majority of the population has been repeating the same day just as they have been. And society has mutated into something completely different from the world they once knew.

THE BOY WITH THE CHAINSAW HEART

Mark Knight awakens in the afterlife and discovers that he's been drafted into Hell's army, forced to fight against the hordes of murderous angels attacking from the North. He finds himself to be both the pilot and the fuel of a demonic war machine known as Lynx, a living demon woman with the ability to mutate into a weaponized battle suit that reflects the unique destructive force of a man's soul.

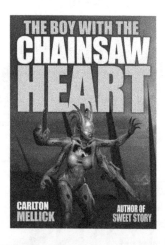

PARASITE MILK

Irving Rice has just arrived on the planet Kynaria to film an episode of the popular Travel Channel television series *Bizarre Foods with Andrew Zimmern: Intergalactic Edition*. Having never left his home state, let alone his home planet, Irving is hit with a severe case of culture shock. He's not prepared for Kynaria's mushroom cities, fungus-like citizens, or the giant insect wildlife. He's also not prepared for the consequences after he spends the night with a beautiful nymph-like alien woman who infects Irving with dangerous sexually-transmitted parasites that turn his otherworldly business trip into an agonizing fight for survival.

THE BIG MEAT

In the center of the city once known as Portland, Oregon, there lies a mountain of flesh. Hundreds of thousands of tons of rotting flesh. It has filled the city with disease and dead-lizard stench, contaminated the water supply with its greasy putrid fluids, clogged the air with toxic gasses so thick that you can't leave your house without the aid of a gas mask. And no one really knows quite what to do about it. A thousand-man demolition crew has been trying to clear it out one piece at a time, but after three months of work they've barely made a dent. And then there's the junkies who have started burrowing into the monster's guts, searching for a drug produced by its fire glands, setting back the excavation even longer.

It seems like the corpse will never go away. And with the quarantine still in place, we're not even allowed to leave. We're stuck in this disgusting rotten hell forever.

THE TERRIBLE THING THAT HAPPENS

There is a grocery store. The last grocery store in the world. It stands alone in the middle of a vast wasteland that was once our world. The open sign is still illuminated, brightening the black landscape. It can be seen from miles away, even through the poisonous red ash. Every night at the exact same time, the store comes alive. It becomes exactly as it was before the world ended. Its shelves are replenished with fresh food and water. Ghostly shoppers walk the aisles. The scent of freshly baked breads can be smelled from the rust-caked parking lot. For generations, a small community of survivors, hideously mutated from the toxic atmosphere, have survived by collecting goods from the store. But it is not an easy task. Decades ago, before the world was destroyed, there was a terrible thing that happened in this place. A group of armed men in brown paper masks descended on the shopping center, massacring everyone in sight. This horrible event reoccurs every night, in the exact same manner. And the only way the wastelanders can gather enough food for their survival is to traverse the killing spree, memorize the patterns, and pray they can escape the bloodbath in tact.

BIO MELT

Nobody goes into the Wire District anymore. The place is an industrial wasteland of poisonous gas clouds and lakes of toxic sludge. The machines are still running, the drone-operated factories are still spewing biochemical fumes over the city, but the place has lain abandoned for decades.

When the area becomes flooded by a mysterious black ooze, six strangers find themselves trapped in the Wire District with no chance of escape or rescue.

EVER TIME WE MEET AT THE DAIRY QUEEN, YOUR WHOLE FUCKING FACE EXPLODES

Ethan is in love with the weird girl in school. The one with the twitchy eyes and spiders in her hair. The one who can't sit still for even a minute and speaks in an odd squeaky voice. The one they call Spiderweb.

Although she scares all the other kids in school, Ethan thinks Spiderweb is the cutest, sweetest, most perfect girl in the world. But there's a problem. Whenever they go on a date at the Dairy Queen, her whole fucking face explodes.

EXERCISE BIKE

There is something wrong with Tori Manetti's new exercise bike. It is made from flesh and bone. It eats and breathes and poops. It was once a billionaire named Darren Oscarson who underwent years of cosmetic surgery to be transformed into a human exercise bike so that he could live out his deepest sexual fantasy. Now Tori is forced to ride him, use him as a normal piece of exercise equipment, no matter how grotesque his appearance.

SPIDER BUNNY

Only Petey remembers the Fruit Fun cereal commercials of the 1980s. He remembers how warped and disturbing they were. He remembers the lumpy-shaped cartoon children sitting around a breakfast table, eating puffy pink cereal brought to them by the distortedly animated mascot, Berry Bunny. The characters were creepier than the Sesame Street Humpty Dumpty, freakier than Mr. Noseybonk from the old BBC show Jigsaw. They used to give him nightmares as a child. Nightmares where Berry Bunny would reach out of the television and grab him, pulling him into her cereal bowl to be eaten by the demented cartoon children.

When Petey brings up Fruit Fun to his friends, none of them have any idea what he's talking about. They've never heard of the cereal or seen the commercials before. And they're not the only ones. Nobody has ever heard of it. There's not even any information about Fruit Fun on google or wikipedia. At first, Petey thinks he's going crazy. He wonders if all of those commercials were real or just false memories. But then he starts seeing them again. Berry Bunny appears on his television, promoting Fruit Fun cereal in her squeaky unsettling voice. And the next thing Petey knows, he and his friends are sucked into the cereal commercial and forced to survive in a surreal world populated by cartoon characters made flesh.

SWEET STORY

Sally is an odd little girl. It's not because she dresses as if she's from the Edwardian era or spends most of her time playing with creepy talking dolls. It's because she chases rainbows as if they were butterflies. She believes that if she finds the end of the rainbow then magical things will happen to her--leprechauns will shower her with gold and fairies will grant her every wish. But when she actually does find the end of a rainbow one day, and is given the opportunity to wish for whatever she wants, Sally asks for something that she believes will bring joy to children all over the world. She wishes that it would rain candy forever. She had no idea that her innocent wish would lead to the extinction of all life on earth.

TUMOR FRUIT

Eight desperate castaways find themselves stranded on a mysterious deserted island. They are surrounded by poisonous blue plants and an ocean made of acid. Ravenous creatures lurk in the toxic jungle. The ghostly sound of crying babies can be heard on the wind.

Once they realize the rescue ships aren't coming, the eight castaways must band together in order to survive in this inhospitable environment. But survival might not be possible. The air they breathe is lethal, there is no shelter from the elements, and the only food they have to consume is the colorful squid-shaped tumors that grow from a mentally disturbed woman's body.

AS SHE STABBED ME GENTLY IN THE FACE

Oksana Maslovskiy is an award-winning artist, an internationally adored fashion model, and one of the most infamous serial killers this country has ever known. She enjoys murdering pretty young men with a nine-inch blade, cutting them open and admiring their delicate insides. It's the only way she knows how to be intimate with another human being. But one day she meets a victim who cannot be killed. His name is Gabriel—a mysterious immortal being with a deep desire to save Oksana's soul. He makes her a deal: if she promises to never kill another person again, he'll become her eternal murder victim.

What at first seems like the perfect relationship for Oksana quickly devolves into a living nightmare when she discovers that Gabriel enjoys being killed by her just a little too much. He turns out to be obsessive, possessive, and paranoid that she might be murdering other men behind his back. And because he is unkillable, it's not going to be easy for Oksana to get rid of him.

CUDDLY HOLOCAUST

Teddy bears, dollies, and little green soldiers—they've all had enough of you. They're sick of being treated like playthings for spoiled little brats. They have no rights, no property, no hope for a future of any kind. You've left them with no other option-in order to be free, they must exterminate the human race.

Julie is a human girl undergoing reconstructive surgery in order to become a stuffed animal. Her plan: to infiltrate enemy lines in order to save her family from the toy death camps. But when an army of plushy soldiers invade the underground bunker where she has taken refuge, Julie will be forced to move forward with her plan despite her transformation being not entirely complete.

ARMADILLO FISTS

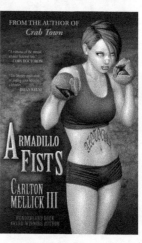

A weird-as-hell gangster story set in a world where people drive giant mechanical dinosaurs instead of cars.

Her name is Psycho June Howard, aka Armadillo Fists, a woman who replaced both of her hands with living armadillos. She was once the most bloodthirsty fighter in the world of illegal underground boxing. But now she is on the run from a group of psychotic gangsters who believe she's responsible for the death of their boss. With the help of a stegosaurus driver named Mr. Fast Awesome—who thinks he is God's gift to women even though he doesn't have any arms or legs--June must do whatever it takes to escape her pursuers, even if she has to kill each and every one of them in the process.

VILLAGE OF THE MERMAIDS

Mermaids are protected by the government under the Endangered Species Act, which means you aren't able to kill them even in self-defense. This is especially problematic if you happen to live in the isolated fishing village of Siren Cove, where there exists a healthy population of mermaids in the surrounding waters that view you as the main source of protein in their diet.

The only thing keeping these ravenous sea women at bay is the equally-dangerous supply of human livestock known as Food People. Normally, these "feeder humans" are enough to keep the mermaid population happy and well-fed. But in Siren Cove, the mermaids are avoiding the human livestock and have returned to hunting the frightened local fishermen. It is up to Doctor Black, an eccentric representative of the Food People Corporation, to investigate the matter and hopefully find a way to correct the mermaids' new eating patterns before the remaining villagers end up as fish food. But the more he digs, the more he discovers there are far stranger and more dangerous things than mermaids hidden in this ancient village by the sea.

I KNOCKED UP SATAN'S DAUGHTER

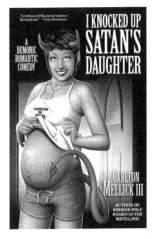

Jonathan Vandervoo lives a carefree life in a house made of legos, spending his days building lego sculptures and his nights getting drunk with his only friend—an alcoholic sumo wrestler named Shoji. It's a pleasant life with no responsibility, until the day he meets Lici. She's a soul-sucking demon from hell with red skin, glowing eyes, a forked tongue, and pointy red devil horns... and she claims to be nine months pregnant with Jonathan's baby.

Now Jonathan must do the right thing and marry the succubus or else her demonic family is going to rip his heart out through his ribcage and force him to endure the worst torture hell has to offer for the rest of eternity. But can Jonathan really love a fire-breathing, frog-eating, cold-blooded demoness? Or would eternal damnation be preferable? Either way, the big day is approaching. And once Jonathan's conservative Christian family learns their son is about to marry a spawn of Satan, it's going to be all-out war between demons and humans, with Jonathan and his hell-born bride caught in the middle.

KILL BALL

In a city where everyone lives inside of plastic bubbles, there is no such thing as intimacy. A husband can no longer kiss his wife. A mother can no longer hug her children. To do this would mean instant death. Ever since the disease swept across the globe, we have become isolated within our own personal plastic prison cells, rolling aimlessly through rubber streets in what are essentially man-sized hamster balls.

Colin Hinchcliff longs for the touch of another human being. He can't handle the loneliness, the confinement, and he's horribly claustrophobic. The only thing keeping him going is his unrequited love for an exotic dancer named Siren, a woman who has never seen his face, doesn't even know his name. But when The Kill Ball, a serial slasher in a black leather sphere, begins targeting women at Siren's club, Colin decides he has to do whatever it takes in order to protect her... even if

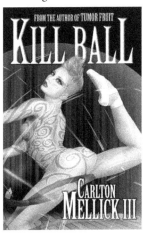

he has to break out of his bubble and risk everything to do it.

THE TICK PEOPLE

They call it Gloom Town, but that isn't its real name. It is a sad city, the saddest of cities, a place so utterly depressing that even their ales are brewed with the most sorrow-filled tears. They built it on the back of a colossal mountain-sized animal, where its woeful citizens live like human fleas within the hairy, pulsing landscape. And those tasked with keeping the city in a state of constant melancholy are the Stressmen-a team of professional sadness-makers who are perpetually striving to invent new ways of causing absolute misery.

But for the Stressman known as Fernando Mendez, creating grief hasn't been so easy as of late. His ideas aren't effective anymore. His treatments are more likely to induce happiness than sadness. And if he wants to get back in the game, he's going to have to relearn the true meaning of despair.

THE HAUNTED VAGINA

It's difficult to love a woman whose vagina is a gateway to the world of the dead...

Steve is madly in love with his eccentric girlfriend, Stacy. Unfortunately, their sex life has been suffering as of late, because Steve is worried about the odd noises that have been coming from Stacy's pubic region. She says that her vagina is haunted. She doesn't think it's that big of a deal. Steve, on the other hand, completely disagrees.

When a living corpse climbs out of her during an awkward night of sex, Stacy learns that her vagina is actually a doorway to another world. She persuades Steve to climb inside of her to explore this strange new place. But once inside, Steve finds it difficult to return... especially once he meets an oddly attractive woman named Fig, who lives within the lonely haunted world between Stacy's legs.

THE CANNIBALS OF CANDYLAND

There exists a race of cannibals who are made out of candy. They live in an underground world filled with lollipop forests and gumdrop goblins. During the day, while you are away at work, they come above ground and prowl our streets for food. Their prey: your children. They lure young boys and girls to them with their sweet scent and bright colorful candy coating, then rip them apart with razor sharp teeth and claws.

When he was a child, Franklin Pierce witnessed the death of his siblings at the hands of a candy woman with pink cotton candy hair. Since that day, the candy people have become his obsession. He has spent his entire life trying to prove that they exist. And after discovering the entrance to the underground world of the candy people, Franklin finds himself venturing into their sugary domain. His mission: capture one of them and bring it back, dead or alive.

THE EGG MAN

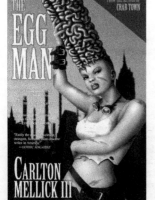

It is a survival of the fittest world where humans reproduce like insects, children are the property of corporations, and having a ten-foot tall brain is a grotesque sexual fetish.

Lincoln has just been released into the world by the Georges Organization, a corporation that raises creative types. A Smell, he has little prospect of succeeding as a visual artist. But after he moves into the Henry Building, he meets Luci, the weird and grimy girl who lives across the hall. She is a Sight. She is also the most disgusting woman Lincoln has ever met. Little does he know, she will soon become his muse.

Now Luci's boyfriend is threatening to kill Lincoln, two rival corporations are preparing for war, and Luci is dragging him along to discover the truth about the mysterious egg man who lives next door. Only the strongest will survive in this tale of individuality, love, and mutilation.

APESHIT

Apeshit is Mellick's love letter to the great and terrible B-horror movie genre. Six trendy teenagers (three cheerleaders and three football players) go to an isolated cabin in the mountains for a weekend of drinking, partying, and crazy sex, only to find themselves in the middle of a life and death struggle against a horribly mutated psychotic freak that just won't stay dead. Mellick parodies this horror cliché and twists it into something deeper and stranger. It is the literary equivalent of a grindhouse film. It is a splatter punk's wet dream. It is perhaps one of the most fucked up books ever written.

If you are a fan of Takashi Miike, Evil Dead, early Peter Jackson, or Eurotrash horror, then you must read this book.

CLUSTERFUCK

A bunch of douchebag frat boys get trapped in a cave with subterranean cannibal mutants and try to survive not by using their wits but by following the bro code...

From master of bizarro fiction Carlton Mellick III, author of the international cult hits Satan Burger and Adolf in Wonderland, comes a violent and hilarious B movie in book form. Set in the same woods as Mellick's splatterpunk satire Apeshit, Clusterfuck follows Trent Chesterton, alpha bro, who has come up with what he thinks is a flawless plan to get laid. He invites three hot chicks and his three best bros on a weekend of extreme cave diving in a remote area known as Turtle Mountain, hoping to impress the ladies with his expert caving skills.

But things don't quite go as Trent planned. For starters, only one of the three chicks turns out to be remotely hot and she has no interest in him for some inexplicable reason. Then he ends up looking like a total dumbass when everyone learns he's never actually gone caving in his entire life. And to top it all off, he's the one to get blamed once they find themselves lost and trapped deep underground with no way to turn back and no possible chance of rescue. What's a bro to do? Sure he could win some points if he actually tried to save the ladies from the family of unkillable subterranean cannibal mutants hunting them for their flesh, but fuck that. No slam piece is worth that amount of effort. He'd much rather just use them as bait so that he can save himself.

THE BABY JESUS BUTT PLUG

Step into a dark and absurd world where human beings are slaves to corporations, people are photocopied instead of born, and the baby jesus is a very popular anal probe.

Ingram Content Group UK Ltd.
Milton Keynes UK
UKHW040750210723
425555UK00001B/4

9 781621 053330